MW01094364

# A Split Second

ALSO BY JANAE MARKS

*From the Desk of Zoe Washington*
*On Air with Zoe Washington*
*A Soft Place to Land*

JANAE MARKS

# A SPLIT SECOND

**Quill Tree Books**
An Imprint of HarperCollinsPublishers

Quill Tree Books is an imprint of HarperCollins Publishers.
A Split Second
Copyright © 2024 by Janae Marks
Interior art © Adobe Stock

Library of Congress Control Number: 2023948431
ISBN 978-0-06-321236-7

Typography by Laura Mock
24 25 26 27 28 LBC 5 4 3 2 1
First Edition

For Jenifer P.,
my true friend since
the very beginning

# Part One

## Elise

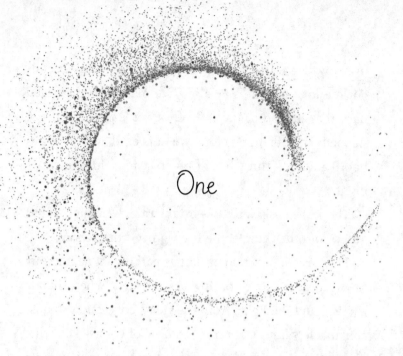

# One

The moon is full, and so is my belly—and my heart.

It's the weekend of our town's annual fall carnival, and I'm here with my best friends, Melinda and Ivy. My twelfth birthday was a few days ago, but I'm celebrating tonight. Rides, fried dough, and my favorite people? I can't think of a better combination.

"What do you think . . . should we go on the Tilt-A-Whirl again?" Ivy shouts above the crowd of people surrounding us.

"Yes!" Melinda immediately agrees.

"I'm in!" I beam at them and adjust the birthday sash

over my fleece jacket. It's one of the presents my friends got me for tonight. They also gave me a plastic jeweled tiara that unfortunately fell off at some point and got stepped on. But not before we squeezed into a photo booth and took three sets of photo strips with me wearing it.

The three of us walk toward the ride, weaving around groups of other kids, some I recognize from school.

The carnival is set up on a huge parking lot next to our town's beach. I love coming here at night when the air is crisp, and the lights from the rides, concession stands, and arcade games flash in a rainbow of colors. The families with younger kids have gone home, and the parents of older kids let them hang out by themselves. It feels like the carnival belongs to my friends and me.

Ivy, Melinda, and I get in line for the ride. When a gust of wind blows, we huddle closer, looping our arms together. I'm in the middle, Ivy rests her head against my right shoulder, and Melinda rests hers against my left. As the line moves, we giggle as we try to stay in this same position while stepping forward. With my friends on either side of me, I feel warm again, but also happy and safe.

We ride two more times, and I scream my guts out.

When we're finally off, the air feels chillier. "I want

something warm to drink," I say. "Like hot chocolate."

"What the birthday girl wants, the birthday girl gets," Ivy singsongs.

I smile, and we head to the nearest concession stand.

"Oh look, they have hot caramel apple cider," Melinda says. "I'm getting that."

We pay for our warm beverages and stand with them for a second while we look for a free table. There's one near the arcade games.

As I sip my hot cocoa, which still needs to cool off, I spot Cora Burroughs taking pictures with a fancy camera. She also goes to our school, and I've known her since we were little kids. Once upon a time we were close friends, but we haven't hung out or spoken much since the fourth grade. I wonder why she's photographing the ring toss game. She stares at the camera screen before turning in our direction. I see her notice my birthday sash, and then we make eye contact. I almost look away but flash a smile instead. She smiles back, making her dimples show.

Then she walks up to me.

"Happy birthday, El—" Cora starts to say.

"Wait, I see something over there," Melinda says, cutting Cora off. "Come look."

Cora stands aside as Ivy gets up and follows Melinda, who's already walking away.

I go after them, pausing first to turn and glance at Cora.

She's staring right at me, but I can't quite read her expression. I say "thanks" before catching up with Ivy and Melinda.

"Eww. I just burped, and it tasted like apple cider," Ivy says.

"Eww!" Melinda says, and we all laugh.

When we get to the Whack-a-Mole game, Melinda points to a bunch of stuffed dragons hanging around it. "You *need* one of those," she says.

The dragons come in different colors, but my favorite is the light blue one with the purple horn and wings. Melinda's right—I love dragons, and this stuffie is so cute.

"Yes!" Ivy says. "We should win one for you."

We finish our drinks. Then we play—and dramatically lose—a few rounds of the game before deciding it must be rigged. Oh well. At least we had fun playing.

By this point, my dad's here to pick us up so we head toward the exit. It's perfect timing because once we're in his car, it starts to rain.

But our night is far from over. We go back to my house for a sleepover. Earlier, Ivy's and Melinda's parents dropped them off and we set everything up in the basement. There are three sleeping bags lined up in a row.

I pull pillows off the couch to make the floor comfier. The coffee table has bowls of my favorite movie snacks: M&M's, Sour Patch Kids, and popcorn. The TV mounted on the wall is ready to play *Spirited Away*.

We change into our pj's, and then Melinda says, "Open my present." She hands me a gift bag.

I reach inside and pull out the third book in the Dragon Island fantasy series, which I've been obsessed with.

"Thank you!" I say.

"Don't you have that one already?" Ivy asks me. "You were reading it the other day."

Ivy is right. I do already have the third book. I went to Sunny's Books, our local bookstore, on the day it was released to get my copy.

"Oh," Melinda says. Her cheeks redden.

"That's okay!" I quickly say. "I don't mind having an extra copy. Promise."

"I got you two other things, too," she mumbles.

I reach back into the gift bag and pull out a book light and a set of bookmarks. One of them has cats wearing glasses, and the other has "I'd Rather Be Reading" in a fun font.

"I love them!" I lean over to hug her. She relaxes a bit and leans into the hug.

Next, I open Ivy's gift. It's a scrapbook that she made

with pictures of the three of us from the summer. She decorated each page inside with stickers and doodles.

"This is amazing!" I say. "You made this all by yourself?"

"Yup!" Ivy smiles proudly.

I glance at Melinda, who's now focused on picking at her sweater. I hope she isn't still upset about the book thing because it was seriously no big deal.

I open the scrapbook to the first page. There's a picture of the three of us from the last day of sixth grade, in front of the big oak tree at school. We had a super fun sleepover that night, too.

"Let's look at the rest together," I say, pulling the girls toward me.

We huddle close and flip through the scrapbook, reminiscing over our favorite pictures. Like the shot of us on towels at the beach. We were in a row, lying on our bellies with our feet up behind us, in matching heart sunglasses that Melinda had gotten. Melinda always finds the cutest accessories.

There's also a picture of us at a pottery painting place, where we decorated mugs. I painted stars on mine, and it now sits on my desk in my room and holds my bookmark collection.

My favorite picture is from the Fourth of July, when

we went to a local park to watch fireworks. We each wore glow stick necklaces and bracelets.

From the photos, you'd never guess that I only started hanging out with them last spring. It looks like we've been friends forever. I hope we only get closer.

Before putting the scrapbook away, I grab one of our photo strips from the carnival. I slip it between two pages of the scrapbook to keep it safe.

Melinda, Ivy, and I talk for a while, and then we decide to get comfy in our sleeping bags and put on the movie. I turn off the main lights, leaving on the color-changing LED lights that Theo, my older brother, hung up around the ceiling. Right now, they're blue and give the room a cool glow.

Mom comes down to check on us sometime after that. "You have everything you need down here?" She crouches next to me, so she doesn't disturb my friends as they watch the movie.

"Yup," I say.

"Good." Then she holds out a small gold gift bag. "By the way, somebody left this present for you on the front porch. It looked like a girl your age."

"Who was it?" I can't think of anyone who'd drop off a gift for me.

"She didn't ring the doorbell, but I got an alert from

the camera. I couldn't see her face on the screen. Maybe there's a card in the bag?"

"I'll check. Thanks."

Mom goes back upstairs, and I open the bag. There's a small forest-green box with a black sticker on top. It has the name of a shop—Daphne's Delights—and a downtown address. I've never been to this store.

I open the box and inside, lying on top of a square piece of cotton, is an oval-shaped necklace. It's silver, with a swirl design etched onto the front, and it's on a delicate silver chain. As I look at it closer, I realize it's a locket. It's pretty. I open it and find a tiny analog clock inside, with the moving hands already set to the correct time. Then I look around the bag, but there isn't a card or gift tag anywhere. They must have forgotten to include their name. I wish I knew who gave this to me. Maybe I can find out when I'm back at school on Monday. In the meantime, I gently place the locket back into its box and set it on the coffee table.

When the movie's over, Ivy, Melinda, and I position our sleeping bags so that they form a circle, with our pillows in the center. We talk about what we want to do when we wake up in the morning. We decide it'll be fun to make chocolate chip pancakes and then brainstorm costume ideas for Halloween.

Eventually we all get quiet, and Melinda's and Ivy's breathing gets heavier as they drift off to sleep. I wonder how late it is, but my phone is already plugged in upstairs in the kitchen, where my parents make my siblings and me leave our electronics at night.

I remember the clock inside my new locket, so I reach for it. It says it's 11:59 and the tiny second hand clicks steadily toward midnight. I lie back down and curl up in my sleeping bag with the locket still in my hand, resting over my heart. Before I know it, sleep is pulling me in, so I close my eyes and let the darkness take over.

When I wake up the next morning, it feels like I just had the deepest sleep of my life. I open my eyes to the sun streaming in through my bedroom windows. All that birthday excitement must've knocked me out.

*Wait a minute.* Why am I back in my bedroom? I lean over to see if Ivy and Melinda are up here, too, but the floor is empty.

Did I come upstairs by myself last night?

When I stand up out of bed, something shifts on my neck. The locket. Weird . . . I remember falling asleep holding it, but not putting it on.

Still groggy, I walk downstairs and check the basement. The girls aren't there either. Neither are our leftover snacks and drink cups. The basement is all cleaned up.

11

Did they go home early? What about our plans for today? And why didn't they say goodbye?

A weird feeling settles in my stomach. Something must've happened between last night and this morning.

But what?

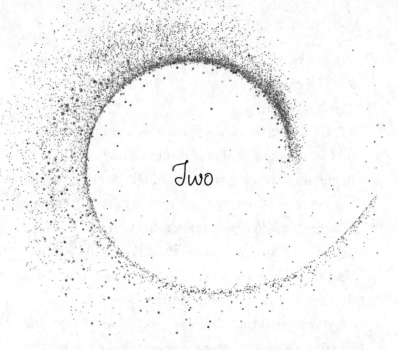

# Two

*I need to find my* phone. I head toward the charging station in the kitchen.

Right away, I notice something strange on the lock screen. Today's date says Monday, April 8.

That isn't right. I turn the phone off, wait a couple of seconds, and then turn it back on. When the home screen loads again, it still says the same date. I go into the date and time settings, which say that they're set automatically. But why would it be wrong? I make sure my phone is connected to Wi-Fi, and it is. Maybe the problem is with our internet.

Then I notice that my sister's tablet has the same date on the lock screen.

My head spins.

There's got to be some explanation. One of my siblings could be playing a joke on me. But usually, we think of silly pranks to play on our parents. Like the time we put googly eyes on all of the containers and cans in the pantry and fridge. Or when we left plastic bugs in the bathroom and laundry room. We haven't done pranks like that in a while, though—not since Shay told Theo and me that she had better things to do with her free time.

I go into my texts to find my group chat with Ivy and Melinda so I can ask them where they went. Our text chain is usually right at the top of my messages, but for some reason it's not there.

I open a new group text and add them to it.

**Where'd you go**

I bite my lower lip and watch the screen, expecting one of them to respond right away. But nobody does. A few minutes later, I send another text.

**Did you go home**
**???**

A minute later, there's still no reply.

"Oh good, you're up."

I jump at the voice, but it's only Mom.

"What?" I ask.

"I was about to get you," she says as she takes the pot off the coffee maker and brings it to the sink to rinse out. "You overslept."

I glance at the time on my phone. It says 7:04, which is pretty early for a Sunday morning.

"Do you know where my friends went?" I ask. "Did their parents pick them up already?"

"What friends?" Mom asks.

"Ivy and Melinda."

"Hmm. I thought you didn't want to talk about those girls," Mom says.

*Huh?*

Then Mom says, "Now hurry up and get dressed for school."

"*School?*" I repeat. "What are you talking about? It's Sunday."

Mom gives me one of her exasperated looks. "I don't have time for games this morning." She dumps scoops of coffee grounds into the filter. "Please get dressed. Dad will drop you off on his way to work."

I stand there, staring at Mom for a second in disbelief.

Has she lost her mind? Or have I lost mine? She seems the same as always as she pours water into the machine and sets it to brew.

Before she can notice that I'm still standing here, I leave the kitchen and go back upstairs. No matter what's going on, it won't be a good idea to make my mom tell me to do something twice.

I peek into my sister Shay's room. She's a high school junior and is dressed in jeans and a teal sweater. One thing's for sure—she wouldn't be up and dressed this early if it wasn't a school day. She's looking at herself in her mirror as she puts on eyeliner.

"I can see you staring at me," she says. "Stop being weird."

I lean against her doorframe. "Did you do something to my phone?"

Shay continues lining her eyelids. "What are you talking about?"

"My phone. It has the wrong date on it."

"Well, I didn't touch it." Then she leans closer to her mirror and lets out a frustrated sigh. "This looks really bad. You're distracting me! Go bother Theo."

If Shay wasn't so focused on getting her makeup perfect, she'd realize that I'm not here to bother her. I'm here because I'm *freaking out*. If this was a few years ago, she would've cared more.

I'm better off talking to Theo, so I go next door to his room. He's a sophomore. His door is closed as usual, but unlike Shay, I know he won't be annoyed if I knock.

"Come in," he says.

When I open the door, Theo is looking at two hoodies, deciding between them. He slips a gray UConn one on and puts the other one back in his dresser drawer.

"What's up?" he asks me.

Unlike Shay's room, which is an explosion of clothes, makeup, and accessories, Theo's room is really tidy. He's the cleanest out of all of us. He makes his bed every morning, keeps his Funko Pop figures lined up neatly on the shelf above his desk, and never keeps dirty clothes on the floor.

"Is today a school day?" I ask.

"I wish it wasn't." He sits on his bed and slips on a pair of socks. "Spring break should really be two weeks long, you know?"

"What?" I ask. *Spring break?*

"What?" Theo repeats, giving me a confused look.

"So, it's actually April . . . ," I say. My heart races.

"Yes." Theo stares at me. "You okay?"

"I'm not sure . . ."

"Elise, is that what you're wearing to school?" Dad

asks from the hallway.

I look down at my pj's, which have strawberries printed all over them. When did I get these?

"No," I say. "I'm getting ready now. I'll be fast."

"Okay." To Theo, he says, "Nice sweatshirt!" UConn is Dad's alma mater.

I take the locket off and leave it on my dresser. Then I shower, brush my teeth, and get dressed.

All the while, I think about how wrong this all is. But I don't know what else to do right now. If today is a school day, then I'll go to school. I'll find Melinda and Ivy there and get to the bottom of this.

"Is everything okay, honey?" Dad asks me once we're in his car. "Shay's normally running behind in the mornings, not you."

He's right. I like to get ready early so I can take my time. I'm usually the first one to get their bowl of cereal for breakfast. I hate feeling rushed.

"I think something's wrong with me," I start, but pause when I realize I don't know how to explain it. Have I really lost my memory? I can't remember anything after the night of the sleepover. Is that how amnesia works?

"Nothing's wrong with you," Dad says. "What you're going through is completely normal. Things like this happen, especially in middle school. Ask Shay. She went through something similar, but she bounced back, and I know you will, too."

Wait, *what?* I have no idea what Dad's talking about.

But before I can ask him about it, he's pulled into the school's parking lot and I have to get out, so I don't miss the first bell.

As we were driving over, I half expected to be the only one at school. Because how is it not Sunday? But there are tons of kids around like any normal weekday. I say bye to Dad and walk into school, trying to explain this to myself. Trying to rationalize why I don't remember anything. I come up short.

Is it really not October anymore? Did I lose—I do the math—*six months* of my memory?

Hopefully when I find Melinda and Ivy, this will all make sense.

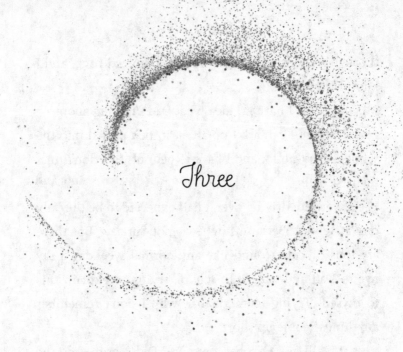

# Three

I search for Melinda and Ivy on the way to my locker, but don't see them anywhere. We don't have any morning classes together, so I check my phone one last time before putting it in my backpack. It still says Monday, April 8, and there are no new messages.

My first class is English, and our teacher, Ms. Harris, always puts the date at the top of the whiteboard, along with a couple of questions to start the class.

April 8. She wrote April 8.

*Is this really happening?*

"Do you have a question, Elise?" Ms. Harris asks me.

Whoops. I did not mean to say that out loud. I shake my head.

"Okay, then," Ms. Harris says to the rest of the class. "Let's get started."

I can barely pay attention throughout the lesson. My stomach's in knots. I think about raising my hand and asking to go to the nurse's office, but what would I say to the nurse? How would I explain this?

No, what I need to do is find my friends. Maybe this is happening to them, too.

I get through my morning classes and rush into the cafeteria as soon as the bell rings.

"Hi, Elise," a voice says. I look over, hoping it's Melinda or Ivy.

But it's Cora Burroughs, staring at me with hopeful eyes.

"Oh, uh. Hey . . ."

I turn to look for the table where I usually eat with Melinda and Ivy. When I spot the two of them, relief washes over me.

"I'm so sorry," I say to Cora. "I've gotta go."

I skip over to the table. "I'm having a crisis," I say as I sit and drop my backpack by my feet. "You're not going to believe this."

Ivy and Melinda stop eating and stare at each other. It's like they're having a silent conversation with their eyes. They won't look at me, and suddenly the air feels thick and tense.

"What's going on?" I ask.

"Let's go find another table," Melinda says quietly to Ivy.

"Good idea," Ivy says back.

They stand up, grab their stuff, and walk away without another word. And without looking back at me.

As I watch them go, my mouth drops open in shock.

They're shutting me out. It's worse than if they'd yelled at me or left a mean note in my locker. At least then I might be able to find out why they're mad at me.

My chest gets really tight, and my head starts to spin.

It's clear now that my memory isn't the only thing I lost.

It looks like, somehow, I lost my best friends, too.

Melinda and I have math together in the afternoon, so when I get to the classroom and see her at her usual seat right in front of my desk, I try to talk to her.

"Mel, what's going on?" I lean forward and keep my voice low. "Why aren't you talking to me?"

At first, it seems like she's not going to answer. Seconds

pass before she turns around.

"Don't try to pretend like you don't know," she finally says, before facing the front of the classroom again.

*What?* I think. *I don't know anything!* I slump back in my chair. I take a few breaths and try to focus on our teacher's word problems.

When class is over, I shouldn't be surprised that Melinda doesn't look back at me when she leaves the room. But it still hurts. When I try to talk to Ivy at the end of the school day at her locker, she ignores me, too.

Something happened the night of the carnival and sleepover. And then something big must've happened to make Melinda and Ivy drop me as a friend. For whatever reason, I can't remember what that is—or anything else from the last six months.

I've got to figure this out. Right away.

As soon as school is over, I go home and run upstairs. Normally I stop in the kitchen for an afternoon snack, but I can't think about eating right now.

In my room, I look around to see if there's anything that explains what's going on. The first thing I search for is my journal. I don't write in it all the time, but I usually take it out whenever I'm sad about something. Losing my best friends would definitely qualify.

I find it in my nightstand and flip to the last page I

wrote on. But the last entry isn't about Melinda or Ivy. It's about Amelia Davis. I wrote it last spring when Amelia, the girl who'd been my best friend since the fourth grade, moved away. I can still see the dried tearstains on the pages where I wrote about how devastated and lonely I felt after she moved. I was a wreck for the rest of the sixth grade.

Then I was assigned an end-of-the-year history project with Ivy. I'd never worked with her before, but she always came across as sweet, bubbly, and energetic. Like a golden retriever. And I knew she was smart because she always participated in class.

Because of that, we got along right away and aced our project. Then she invited me to hang out with her and Melinda at her house. I was nervous about that because I knew she and Melinda were besties and I didn't want to be a third wheel.

I could tell that Melinda wasn't sure at first about having me around. But she seemed to warm up to me, especially once I showed them the candy salad I'd brought over. It was a candy combination that Amelia and I had come up with—gummy bears, Sour Patch Kids, mini Starburst, peach rings, and Swedish Fish. We ate it in the dance studio in Ivy's basement. It's actually her mom's studio, where she teaches ballet classes to kids. It has a separate entrance and a bathroom, too. One wall is all mirrors, with ballet barres mounted to them. The floor is all black and kind of springy, like it wouldn't hurt if you fell on it.

Ivy likes all kinds of dance, so instead of playing classical ballet music, she turned on an upbeat song. Then Melinda suggested that Ivy teach us a routine. Ivy loved this idea and taught us some simple moves. I kept messing up at first, but eventually got it. We looked amazing, and it was so much fun! By the end, my face hurt from laughing so much.

It was the first time that I felt like I might be okay with Amelia gone, even though I still really missed her.

Now I flip through the rest of the journal to make sure I didn't write about Melinda and Ivy somewhere else. But there's nothing. I toss the journal on my bed and keep searching my room.

I check all over my desk and in the drawers for anything that can tell me what happened with Melinda and Ivy—like notes from either of them, or receipts showing where I've been lately. I also check in my closet and in bags I might have used recently. But I can't find a single clue. It's like Melinda and Ivy have been erased from my life. The pictures of us that were pinned to the bulletin board above my desk and taped to the edges of my dresser mirror are gone. I have no idea where they are. I don't see the scrapbook Ivy gave me for my birthday either.

I check my phone again. Besides the original group text being gone, so are all my photos. Did I get a new phone? I turn it around in my hand and it looks the same as I remember. It's in the same case, too.

Feeling defeated, I plop down on my bed and stare around the room, wishing for an explanation to appear in front of my eyes.

Then I spot the locket on my dresser and pick it up. Why is that still here from the sleepover night, but Ivy's scrapbook is missing?

I never even got the chance to find out who this locket came from, though that feels like the least of my problems now.

I rub it between my fingers and go over everything that happened since this morning.

The next thing I know, Shay is poking me and telling me that dinner is ready. I must've fallen asleep. I get up and trudge downstairs to eat with my family.

"How was your day, Elise?" Dad asks me at some point during the meal. "Are you feeling better after this morning?"

"Not really," I admit.

"What happened this morning?" Shay asks, and I

wonder why she suddenly cares now and not when I was panicking in her room.

"You know my friends Ivy and Melinda?" I ask the table.

"I thought you weren't friends with them anymore," Theo says.

"About that . . . Do you know why I stopped hanging out with them? I mean, did I tell you?"

"Not me," Shay says.

"Me neither," Theo says.

"I asked you about it at one point," Mom says. "But you said you didn't want to talk about it. So, I left it at that."

I'm disappointed that Mom didn't pry. She *always* pries, and the one time she doesn't is when I needed her to.

I nod. "I have another weird question. Have you ever, like, lost a huge chunk of time before? Out of nowhere?"

"What's this about?" Dad asks. "Did something happen at school?"

I look around the table and all eyes are on me. They're looking at me like I'm making zero sense.

Because none of this makes sense.

"Actually, never mind." I look down at my plate.

The conversation shifts to something else, but I barely pay attention.

Normally, I spend the hour after dinner finishing up homework, so that's what I do. It's harder than usual, and I realize it's because I don't remember anything that was taught in school over the last six months. My stress multiplies with each task.

By the time I'm getting ready for bed, I've decided that this whole day must be a bad dream. It's the only explanation. I'm in the middle of some strange stress nightmare and when I wake up, everything will be back to normal. It'll be the day after the fall carnival again, I'll be back in my sleeping bag in the basement, and Ivy and Melinda will still be my best friends.

This has got to be the most detailed, strangest dream I've ever had but maybe it's from all that extra sugar from that night. Or maybe there was something in that hot chocolate.

I drift off to sleep as soon as my head hits the pillow.

When I wake up the next morning, I'm still in my bed.

No.

My room looks the same as I left it the night before—a mess from tearing it apart, looking for clues.

To make sure, I run down to the kitchen to check my phone. Now it says April 9.

This isn't a nightmare. It's really happening. I really lost six months of time, somehow.

I brace myself against the kitchen counter as blood rushes to my head, making me dizzy.

I need to find out what happened, especially with Melinda and Ivy. And then I will do whatever I can to set things right.

I'll get my life back.

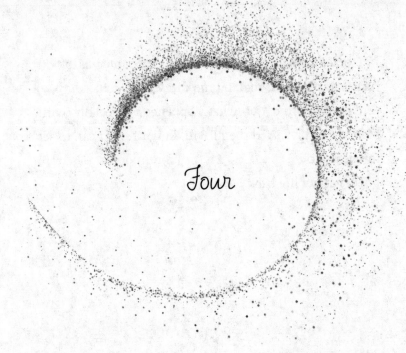

# Four

Since it's apparently Tuesday, I get ready for school like normal. But once I'm there, I'm in a daze. I go to my locker to exchange books, and realize I forgot my lunch bag at home. Guess I'll have to buy lunch today. I check the small pouch in the front pocket of my backpack and see that the emergency cash my parents make me carry is still there.

For the first few class periods, I go through the motions, hoping that at some point, a light will switch on in my brain and I'll remember everything again.

No such luck.

"Elise," a deep voice says when I'm walking to the

cafeteria. I turn toward it, and a teacher with wavy brown hair, black glasses, and a pink polo shirt is staring at me. He's one of the art teachers. I haven't been in his class before, but kids call him Mr. G. He's one of the younger teachers at our school, which makes him one of the more popular ones, too.

*Am I in trouble?*

"Yup?" I squeak out.

"We missed you at photography club yesterday." He gives a warm smile. "I hope everything is okay."

I almost laugh because *nothing* is okay.

"Photography club?" I blink at him a few times. Since when am I in photography club?

He nods. "Your photo essay is coming along great so far. I can't wait to see how you finish it."

*Photo essay?*

He's expecting a response, so I stammer out, "Oh. Right." Then, "I'm fine. Thanks."

"Good. Hope you'll be back next week, then." He flashes another smile before turning and walking away.

I've never been in photography club. At least, I wasn't back in October. I must've joined sometime since then. I add this to my mental list of clues. It's just weird because normally I'm not into artsy extracurricular activities. Or any extracurricular activities. While my other classmates play sports, I usually go to the library to find new books to read.

In the cafeteria, I get in line to buy lunch. Across the room, Ivy and Melinda are sitting at our regular table again, eating and chatting.

A lump forms in my throat. How could our friendship have fallen apart? Things were so great between us the last I remember. I think about the scrapbook Ivy gave me for my birthday—all the happy memories it contained. Plus, the photo strip from the carnival. How could we have been so close when all those pictures were taken, but now they can't stand to look at me?

When I get to the front of the lunch line, I skip past the mystery meat loaf and grab a bowl of macaroni and cheese and an apple. I pay for them, and then walk a few steps with my tray before realizing that I don't know where to sit. I can try to talk to Ivy and Melinda again, but I don't think that'll go well. I can't handle them shutting me out a second time. I could spend lunch hiding in the library instead, but you're not allowed to bring food in there. I'm pretty hungry right now since I skipped breakfast this morning.

I peer around the cafeteria to see if I can join another table. There are plenty of free seats, but not next to anyone I know well. Won't it be weird to sit at a random table where everyone else there is good friends?

I wish Amelia were here. I wish she never moved away.

Suddenly I feel frozen in place. I don't know where else to eat if I leave, but I also don't know where to eat if I stay. I have nowhere to go and nobody to sit with.

The words ping-pong around in my brain. *I have nobody.*

"Elise?"

I spin around, surprised to hear my name. It's Cora. She's holding her own tray with mac and cheese, except she chose a banana instead of an apple.

It's like I manifested her. This girl whose dimples show when she smiles, which she's doing right now. This girl who used to know me, once upon a time.

"Hey." I exhale.

"Do you . . . want to sit together?" Cora asks. "There are a couple empty seats over there."

My stomach answers with a growl before I can get the words out. "Sure. That'd be great."

We sit down and I practically inhale my mac and cheese.

When I glance up at Cora again, she's looking at me with an amused expression. I notice that she's eating her food at a much more normal speed.

"Sorry," I say, pushing my now-empty bowl to the side of the tray. I pick up the apple and roll it around in my hand. "I was too stressed to eat breakfast this morning, so I was starving."

"That's okay," Cora says. "What were you stressed about? Only if you feel like talking about it."

I take sips of my water while I think of what to say. "Just some stuff with my friends. That's why I'm not sitting with them right now."

I can still see Melinda and Ivy from here. Their backs are to me, but Melinda's shoulders shake as she giggles, and Ivy reaches over to offer her a chip from her bag.

They look normal, like nothing's changed. Like they don't miss me at all. Like I was never part of their group to begin with.

The mac and cheese churns in my stomach, so I gulp some more water. Hopefully I can figure all of this out so I'm back to sitting with them soon.

I wonder who Cora normally sits with at lunch. We're not the only ones at this table, but the other kids here are talking among themselves. Now that I think about it, I don't know who Cora normally hangs out with.

When we were friends in elementary school, we usually hung out by ourselves. Or with both of our families. That's because our moms became friends first, when we were little. They met at the library when they each brought us to story time. They sat next to each other and started chatting about mom stuff. After that, they would take us to the playground, or our families would get together for dinner or game nights. Eventually, Cora and I started kindergarten at the same school, and we also went to each other's birthday parties for several years.

Then the pandemic started at the end of the third grade, and suddenly we were both stuck at home. Our families got together for one socially distanced outdoor barbecue over the summer, and we tried video chatting a few times. But it wasn't ever the same as hanging out in person. When we were allowed to go back to school that fall, Cora wasn't in my class, but Amelia was. Amelia and I bonded over our favorite books and graphic novels and ended up starting our own book club. Our friendship grew from there.

I never meant to stop being friends with Cora. We just sort of drifted apart.

"What's going on with Ivy and Melinda?" Cora asks.

I wonder how she knows what friends I'm talking about, since I didn't mention their names. But then I remember that she saw me with them at the carnival, and probably noticed us around school.

"Honestly, I don't know," I say. "They're mad at me. Like, all of a sudden."

I actually don't know how long it's been. Maybe it's only sudden to me.

"That stinks," Cora says. "I'm sorry."

I shrug. "It's not your fault."

Cora stares at her banana for a second before unpeeling it and taking a bite. "Remember when we used to make fluff and banana sandwiches? We loved them until we didn't."

"Oh yeah." I'd forgotten about that. Sometimes we added Nutella, too. But then one day it was like we'd eaten one sandwich too many and couldn't stand the taste anymore.

"It was fun, right?" Cora asks. "When we used to be friends?"

I'm about to say yes when the bell rings, signaling the end of lunch. I throw my backpack on and pick up my lunch tray.

Cora leans down to grab her water bottle from her backpack.

"Thanks for eating lunch with me today," I say.

"We should do it again tomorrow," Cora says.

When she stands back up, I notice that a necklace has slipped out from under her shirt.

Not a necklace. A *locket*. With the same engraving as the one I have at home.

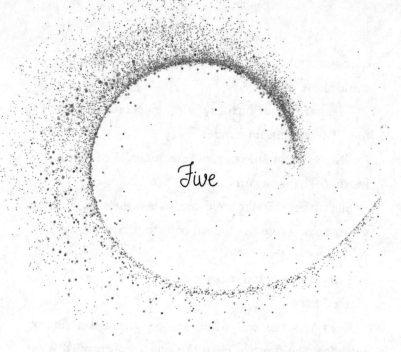

# Five

I glance at the locket again, trying not to seem too obvious.

"Are you coming?" Cora asks.

I follow her to the area where we can throw away our trash and leave our lunch trays.

"Can I see your necklace?" I ask once we're in the hall-way.

Cora looks down. "This? Sure." She leans closer so I can get a better look. It is the exact same oval locket as mine, with the same swirl design.

"This is going to sound strange, but did you give me

the same locket?" Now I wish I'd worn mine today so I could show her.

"Yeah. For your birthday." Cora raises her eyebrows at me. "Do you not remember?"

"No—I mean, of course I remember," I lie. "I just . . . I love it. Thanks again."

She smiles. "You're welcome." Then she says, "I better get to class before the second bell rings. See you later?"

"Yeah. See you."

I rush to class and make it into my seat before I can be marked late.

Cora was the one who gave me the locket for my birthday. She must've been the one who dropped it off on my porch.

*Why?*

We haven't celebrated each other's birthdays in years. Even our moms don't really get together anymore. So why did she decide to give me a birthday gift now? Or, back in October?

Maybe this has something to do with why Ivy and Melinda aren't talking to me anymore. Did Cora and I become friends again during the months I can't remember?

I can't keep living like this, not knowing what happened to me. There has to be an explanation for my memory loss. Maybe I hit my head, and this is from a concussion. But my head doesn't hurt at all. When I feel around the back of it for a bump, there isn't one.

Maybe I had a stroke. Can kids have strokes?

When I get home after school, I start researching memory loss. On my laptop, I scroll through multiple websites, and immediately rule out causes like old age and substance abuse. Apparently, stress, depression, and anxiety can make you forget things. I kind of know what those feel like, but right before I lost my memory, I was happy. Things were finally going well again since Amelia moved away.

I read about traumatic brain injuries, which don't seem likely since my head doesn't seem injured at all. And then I read about brain cancer and become convinced that I have a tumor.

What if I'm dying?

*Breathe, Elise,* I tell myself. I close all my open tabs and take a few calming breaths, like our PE teacher has us do at the start of every class.

I don't have cancer. Probably. And honestly, it doesn't feel like there's anything physically wrong with me. Except for the memory thing, I feel totally normal.

As weird as it sounds, it doesn't even feel like I lost my memory. More that . . . somehow . . . I jumped ahead in time. Like, I went to bed the night of the sleepover in October and magically woke up on a different date. Like time travel or something. But I didn't ask for this to happen.

I open a new tab and search for articles about time travel. The first few results are articles from NASA and university websites with headlines like: "Is Time Travel Possible?" I skim through a few of them, expecting to read that time travel isn't possible. But that's not what they say. They talk about the speed of light and Einstein's theory of relativity, and how it supports the existence of some form of time travel. Just not the kind with time machines. A lot of it goes over my head.

I scroll some more and find a website listing the best time-travel movies. And a news site saying that a cell phone found in a painting from the 1800s proves time travel exists. And a website listing "Time-Travel Spells."

Spells? Like magical spells? Whether or not magic exists is a whole other rabbit hole that I don't want to go down.

I close the window, and then my laptop, feeling no closer to understanding what happened to me.

During dinner that night, I try to see if my family knows anything that could help me.

"Do you remember Cora Burroughs?" I ask Mom.

"Of course," she says. "Can you pass me the salad dressing?"

I hand it to her. "I ate lunch with her today."

40

Mom smiles at this. "That's nice. How's she doing?"

"Good." Then I ask, "Have you seen her recently?"

If Cora and I became friends again, maybe she's been over here lately.

"I haven't," Mom says. "But I should text her mom. We haven't caught up in a while."

"Have any of you seen her lately?" I ask the rest of the table. Dad, Shay, and Theo had been talking about something else.

"Seen who?" Dad asks.

"Cora Burroughs," I say.

"Oh, Cora," Dad says. "I think I saw her when I dropped you at school."

"I haven't seen her," Theo says. "But I'm also not sure I remember what she looks like. . . ."

"Isn't she the one you did the friendship bracelet stand with when you were little?" Shay asks. "You made all my friends buy them. I think I might still have mine somewhere in my room."

"What don't you still have in your room?" Theo asks under his breath.

"What does that mean?" Shay asks.

Theo shrugs. "Just that you could stand to do some decluttering in there."

"Not everyone's a neat freak like you," Shay says.

"Listen, I can help you," Theo says. "*Let me help you.*"

Shay grimaces. "Stay away from my room!"

"All right, enough with the bickering," Dad says. "Though Theo's right, Shay. Your room could use some work."

"Why are you all attacking me?" Shay asks.

"Nobody's attacking you, honey," Mom says.

I zone them out and think about the friendship bracelet stand with Cora. I'd totally forgotten about it. It was the summer between second and third grade, and our families had a joint garage sale. Cora's parents brought a bunch of their old stuff over, and we set everything up on our driveway and in our garage.

Shay wanted to be in charge of making sure all of the items were displayed nicely, so people were more likely to buy them. Then her friends came over and they hung out on the lawn. Theo was our cashier. He sat at a table with a money box and took the job very seriously. Our parents talked to the potential customers and set prices for everything.

Since Cora and I weren't in charge of anything, I suggested we make a lemonade stand.

Cora liked the idea but said we should also sell friendship bracelets. She brought over the supplies to make loom bracelets out of tiny rubber bands. So, our stand had pitchers of freshly squeezed lemonade that we sold for a dollar a cup, as well as customized friendship brace-lets for three dollars. We let the customers pick the color combinations for their bracelets. By the end of the day, we ran out of lemonade and sold almost twenty bracelets. We were so proud of our earnings that we convinced our parents to take us out for ice cream.

If my family hadn't noticed her around lately, then either Cora and I haven't actually started hanging out again, or it's only been at school.

I wish I could remember either way.

After dinner, Shay, Theo, and I clear the table, while Mom and Dad put the leftovers away in the fridge. Shay starts talking about junior prom, and Theo says he thinks a junior might like him, so if things work out maybe he'll go to the prom, too. Shay isn't happy about that, so they bicker some more before Mom makes them stop.

One thing becomes clear as I head back to my room: I'm the only one in this family who went through this time jump. Everyone else is acting like everything is normal. Also, even though I don't remember anything that happened over the last few months, it seems like to everyone else, I was still here.

I was skeptical that something magical or supernatural could've caused this, but right now, it's starting to feel much more possible.

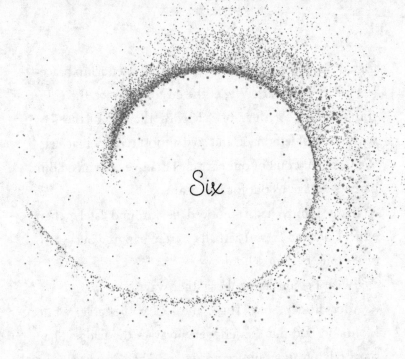

## Six

Now that I know Cora gave me the locket, I have so many questions. Why did she give me a birthday gift in the first place, and why a locket matching hers? Did we become friends again before or after I stopped hanging out with Melinda and Ivy? I can't ask Cora any of this without her thinking I'm weird for not remembering. But maybe if I go to the shop where she bought the necklace—Daphne's Delights—I'll find answers. Maybe I've even been there before and walking around the shop will unlock a memory.

I make sure to wear my locket on Friday morning.

"Can you drive me somewhere after school? Please?"

I ask Shay while she's fishing through the container of granola bars in our pantry to find her favorite flavor.

"Depends," she says. "Where do you need to go?"

"Downtown. There's a store I want to check out."

"What store?" Shay asks.

"Daphne's Delights," I say.

"Is that the store that smells like incense when you walk by?"

"I don't know. I've never been there." At least, not that I can remember. "Can you drive me?" I ask again.

Shay shrugs. "Sure. I'm going to meet Riley down there anyway."

Our town's downtown is a cluster of streets that have shops, restaurants, and my favorite: an independent bookstore called Sunny's Books. It's run by a woman named Beth who named the shop after her yellow lab, Sunny. The dog is usually in the store with her. Sunny's getting older so she spends a lot of time in the dog bed nook that was built into the cash register desk. But she always welcomes pets and ear scratches.

Normally Sunny's Books is my first stop whenever I go downtown. They put out new books every single Tuesday, so there's always something new to look at. I can't afford books all the time, but I'll buy them whenever I can, and add other titles to a list on my phone. Sometimes

45

Beth gives me advance copies of upcoming books that she gets from publishers. Our library is on the other side of our downtown area, so I borrow books all the time, too.

Today, though, I open my phone's map to find out exactly where Daphne's Delights is. It looks like it's two blocks down from the bookstore, next to a boutique clothing store.

When I find it, I have to stop in front and take it all in. The building's brick exterior matches the other ones on this street, but the window display makes it feel different—moodier. The awning is forest green, with "Daphne's Delights" written in gold script, the font matching the sticker from the gift box. The front window has several large crystals on display, as well as candles and some jewelry. When I peer inside, there doesn't seem to be any other customers, but I see someone standing at the register.

*It's just a store,* I tell myself when nerves start to appear. *A store that could help me get my lost time back.* Before I can change my mind, I walk to the door and pull it open. Several bells chime as the door slams closed behind me. The noises make me jump.

When I imagined what an employee of a place like this might look like, I expected someone with long hair or braids, wearing flowing outfits and big hoop earrings.

But this lady is nothing like that. Her skin is pale, and her hair is short, very short—like a pixie cut. It's also a bright silvery color. She doesn't look old enough to have naturally gray hair, so she must dye it. She's wearing a black dress—probably the only thing about her look that I'm not surprised about—but it's not loose or flowy. She's also wearing a black motorcycle jacket and a couple of gold necklaces and bracelets.

She looks . . . *cool*. Interesting.

And she's staring right at me.

I stand there, frozen in place.

"Welcome," she says with an easy smile. "I'm Daphne, the owner. Can I help you with anything?" Her voice is soft and higher pitched than I would've thought. She speaks slowly, like she's in no rush. And why would she be when there's nobody else in here?

Immediately, all the things I planned to say fly out of my head. "No, thanks. I'm just looking."

Daphne smiles. "Sure. Let me know if you need help finding anything."

I turn to look around. The shop is even moodier inside. The walls and ceiling are painted a deep shade of blue, like the color of the sky at midnight. There are fairy lights strung around the room and in mason jars on shelves behind the cash register. I look up, and there are star constellations painted on the ceiling in gold paint. Light, ambient music plays from hidden speakers. I have to admit, it feels pretty magical in here.

I spot a bookshelf on the far wall, so of course I go check that out first. Half the shelves have books, and the other half have candles and other trinkets. I start by browsing through the book titles.

*Crystals from Actinolite to Zoisite*

*The Little Book of Dreams*

*Spells and Rituals for All Occasions*

These are not . . . the kinds of books I usually go for.

I spin around and notice a necklace display. There are necklaces with charms for each astrological sign, and some with healing crystal pendants. Then I spot the lockets. The first one I open has a tiny compass inside. My eyes eventually land on the same silver oval locket that I'm wearing, with the swirl pattern on the front.

"Do you like lockets?"

I jump at Daphne's voice and realize she's now standing right next to me. She was so quiet, it's like she floated over here.

"These are really beautiful, right?" Daphne asks. "There's a clock inside, and a space for a tiny photo."

I clear my throat. "They're pretty. Actually." I pause to pull the locket out from under my shirt. "I have one.

48

A girl at school . . . a friend . . . gave it to me. There's no photo inside, though."

Recognition fills Daphne's face. "Ah, yes. I remember selling a pair of lockets to a young girl like you. She got one for herself, too, right?"

I nod.

"Well, I'm glad you like it. It looks beautiful on you."

"Thanks." I glance around the room. "What kind of shop is this?"

"We're a gift shop," Daphne says. "Besides jewelry, I sell crystals, tarot cards, candles, and some other magical trinkets."

"Magical?" I ask. "Like, pretend magic?" I think of those sleight of hand tricks that magicians do at parties.

"Not *pretend*, no," Daphne says.

"You believe in that? Actual magic?"

Daphne looks completely serious when she says, "Of course. Magic is simply another form of energy that's all around us, like fire and electricity. It's about how you manipulate it."

Normally, I'd think everything Daphne just said was nonsense. I love reading novels involving magic, but I told myself it was all make-believe and fantasy. Now, though, with this freaky time jump, I'm not so sure. Maybe magic does have something to do with it. I'm tempted to ask

Daphne if anything like this has happened to her before but clam up before the words come out.

Instead, I say, "This might be a weird question, but have you . . ." I pause for a second. "Have you seen me in here before? Like, have I come to your shop before?"

The way Daphne looks at me, it's like she was expecting this question.

"No. You haven't." She taps the spot next to her right eye and says, "I never forget a face."

That's disappointing. I guess this place has nothing to do with my time jump if I've never been here before.

Now that I have the answer I need, I'm ready to go. But I feel like I should buy something first, since Daphne has been so nice in answering my questions. Something small, just so I'm not leaving empty-handed. I walk over to the candle section. There are packs of "magic spell candles" in different colors. Then I see some scented soy candles. The small ones in metal tins are $15. I still have another $20 bill in my backpack. I open a few of the candles to sniff them, and decide I like the one that smells like sage, pine, and rain the best. I bring the candle to the counter, where Daphne is now standing on the other side of the register, waiting for me.

"Beautiful choice," Daphne says as she wraps the candle tin in tissue paper and puts it in a small brown paper bag with the Daphne's Delights logo stamped on it. "Cash or card?"

"Cash." I reach into my backpack pocket and pull it out.

"Thanks," I say as she hands me the bag and my change.

"It was nice to meet you, Elise," Daphne says as I'm walking out. "Please come again soon."

I'm halfway down the block when I realize it.

I never told Daphne my name.

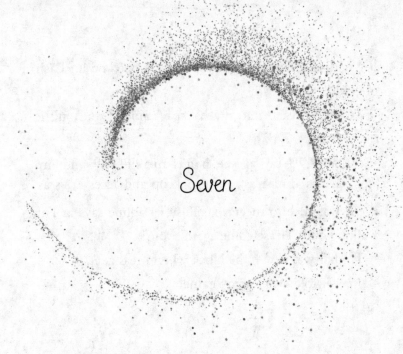

# Seven

Weekends used to be my favorite time because I could fill the days reading books and hanging out with my friends.

But when Friday night rolls around, I'm not excited. Instead, I feel lost. My head is still spinning from the events of the last week and all the questions I can't answer. Whether or not magic is real. Why my friends won't talk to me. Is my memory completely shot? Like, did I tell Daphne my name and forgot? I've somehow lost time, lost friends, and it feels like maybe I'm losing my mind, too. Everything feels out of control.

If this was a Saturday last summer, I'd text with Ivy

and Melinda and make plans. We might get our parents to drop us off downtown so we could get bubble tea and shop around. Or meet at CVS, load up on snacks, and go back to one of our houses to watch movies all day. Or look online for ideas to give each other makeovers. Melinda has almost as much makeup and accessories as Shay.

But nobody's texting me. The thought of Melinda and Ivy hanging out without me makes my body feel heavy. So, after breakfast, I curl back into bed and fall asleep for a while.

Sometime later, Mom checks on me.

"Are you feeling sick?" She comes over to my bed and checks my forehead. "You don't seem warm."

"I'm fine." I sit up. "Just tired."

"I can make you some tea," Mom says.

"Okay."

Mom leaves and comes back ten minutes later with a mug of honey vanilla chamomile tea. My favorite. The fact that my favorite tea flavor hasn't changed is more comforting than the tea itself. I sip it while staring around my room, blinking away sleep.

I wish I knew how I spent weekends during the time I lost. Probably reading. I see a few books on the shelves in my bedroom that I don't recognize. From the creases in the paperback spine, they look like they've been read. I even find a Sunny's Books receipt in one of them, which I must've used as a bookmark. The receipt shows that I bought the book during my lost time. It's weird to think that there's this other version of myself that existed during those six months, making decisions, reading books, living my life.

It's like when I've woken from a deep sleep and can tell I had vivid dreams overnight, but the memories dissolve as soon as I'm fully alert again. Dream Elise did all these things during my lost time—in what feels like an alternate reality—and now I have to piece it all together.

At the very least I can find out what Dream Elise read during that time. From the pile of books, it seems like she was into the same kinds of fantasy and adventure stories that I normally go for.

I grab one and spend the rest of the weekend absorbed in another world.

On Monday I decide to go to the photography club meeting after school. It might help me uncover some clues about what happened during my lost time, since unlike Daphne's Delights, I know I spent time there. At least according to Mr. G. Maybe there are even pictures from my lost time that I can look through. Mr. G said I was working on a photo essay. I don't know what that means so I Google it before school.

One photography website says that a photo essay tells a story through a series of images. *Huh.* I'm curious to see what kind of story Dream Elise wanted to tell. Especially since the only kind of camera I've ever used is the one on my phone.

I'm super nervous when it's time to head over. What if I don't recognize anyone and don't know what to do? What if there's some routine that the club always follows, and I end up looking ridiculous because I don't remember any of it? What if I'm supposed to use some fancy camera and I end up breaking it? I don't even know what kind of photography we do. Does our school have a darkroom? I have no idea how to use a darkroom.

When I get to Mr. G's classroom door, I'm super close to turning around and forgetting this whole plan. Who needs memories or friends? I can just read for the rest of my life.

But then I spot Cora sitting at a desk inside and breathe the hugest sigh of relief. Of course she's in this club, too.

She looks up from a pile of pictures in front of her and sees me. Immediately she breaks out in a grin. "Hey!"

I smile back, so glad to have a friend here. My only friend right now. I wonder, did we become friends again after I joined photography club, or did I join photography club because we became friends again?

I walk over to her. "I'm happy you're here." Then I realize she's probably always here. "I mean, I'm happy I'm here. Since I missed last week." I give a nervous laugh.

"Me, too."

"Elise!" Mr. G says from across the room. He comes over and stands next to me and Cora. "I'm glad you could make it today. Go ahead and grab your folder, and let's see what you've got so far."

Oh no. What folder? And where do I grab it from?

"Sure," I say, and my eyes scan the room for where the folders might be held.

"Over there," Cora says, nodding toward a table next to Mr. G's desk.

"Right." I walk over and flip through the folders until I see my name. It's my handwriting on the front of the folder, but I don't remember writing it. This is so creepy.

I carry it back to the desks and sit in the one next to Cora. I open the folder and see printouts of a few pictures. I immediately recognize what's in them—Sunny's Books. There's a shot of Sunny in her dog bed nook, an angled shot of the middle grade bookshelves, and a close-up of a paper bag with the store's logo printed on it.

"Our beloved town bookstore," Mr. G says, then his expression becomes more pensive. "Remind me, what is the story you're trying to tell here?"

My mind draws a blank. What story would I try to tell with pictures of the bookstore—how much I love books?

"It's about . . ." I swallow and try to think fast. "Community." It's the first thing that pops into my head. "You know, since it's a community bookstore, it brings people together . . . in the . . . community."

I start to sweat, but Mr. G doesn't seem to notice. "I love that," he says with an earnest nod. "Did you take any new pictures in the last two weeks?"

I shake my head.

"That's okay. How about you look through what you have and think about what else you might take photos of, to really fill in this story you're telling. Sound good?"

"Yup."

"Great." He claps once. "Keep up the good work."

A kid across the room asks for help with the photo printer, so Mr. G flits over there like he's a bumblebee homing in on a flower. He seems to have that kind of energy as he darts around the classroom from one student to the next.

I exhale, glad that I was able to somewhat pull off that I knew what I was talking about. All I can say is thank goodness Dream Elise likes the same stuff as me.

I glance over at the photos in front of Cora to see what

her essay's about. There's a shot of a stage with set pieces on it, and then another picture of a woman in a costume putting makeup on in front of a mirror. Her essay must have something to do with the theater.

I look through my own photos again and feel disoriented. I have no idea when I took these pictures, or what I should be doing right now. Would it be weird if I just . . . walked out?

"Can I ask you a random question?" Cora suddenly asks.

"Sure," I say.

Cora leans in closer to me so nobody else can hear her. Her breath smells like strawberry gum. "Is something wrong with your memory?"

An electric shock shoots down my spine.

Cora knows something's up.

*How on earth am I going to answer her?*

# Eight

*Cora stares at me, waiting* for me to respond.

I try to keep my voice even when I ask, "What do you mean?"

"The other day you didn't remember that I gave you your locket, and now you seem really confused about what's going on in photography club," Cora says. "When you looked at your photo essay pictures, it was like you'd never seen them before, even though you're the one who took them."

My mind races with possible responses. She'll think I'm nuts if I tell her I jumped ahead in time. Time travel isn't real! Or, if it is real—if that's what happened to me—people don't usually believe in it. I don't know Cora well enough anymore to know if she'll believe me.

At the same time, I really want to talk to someone about this. I really want to tell Cora. I can't keep dealing with this alone. She's been nothing but nice, and we have shared history.

I trusted her when we were little kids. Maybe I can trust her again.

Then again, that was ages ago, and we grew apart. I barely know her now.

Finally, I blurt out, "I'm fine."

Cora is the only friend I have right now, and I can't risk losing her because of some freak event that happened to me. That I don't even understand yet.

"Are you sure?" Cora asks. "I won't judge."

I sigh. This is my chance to finally admit to someone what's been going on.

"Actually, can we talk after we're done here?" My eyes peer around the room before focusing back on her. She stares at me so intently. "Alone?"

"Sure," Cora says. "If you want, you can come over to my house."

I nod and hope I'm not making a huge mistake. I remind myself that she's the one who gave me a necklace from Daphne's Delights, a shop that sells magical trinkets.

Maybe she believes in supernatural stuff. Maybe she'll believe me.

I spend the rest of photography club hoping that she will.

Cora lives only a couple of streets away from school, so I text my dad to ask if he can pick me up at her house instead. Since he knows Cora and her family from before, I'm pretty sure he'll agree.

He does, and says he'll pick me up in thirty minutes. That'll give me enough time to tell Cora everything. If it goes badly, I'll tell her I was joking, go home, and then have a serious talk with my parents about homeschooling.

Cora and I leave the school building and walk across the field toward the street. We're quiet at first while I build up the courage to tell Cora about the time jump. Maybe she can sense my nerves because she doesn't ask me to talk. Or she might be waiting for us to get to her house.

I stare at the different houses and lawns as we pass by. A lot of them have potted flowers on their stoops. Some still have Easter decorations up, which reminds me that I missed so many holidays. Halloween was the week after the fall carnival. Ivy, Melinda, and I were going to go trick-or-treating in matching outfits, but we were supposed to brainstorm ideas the morning after our sleepover. I wonder what we came up with, and if I still went out with them. Or maybe our friendship fell apart before Halloween. I'll have to try to look for photos.

I missed several family birthdays. Plus, all of winter. Not to mention Thanksgiving and my favorite holiday, Christmas. The week between Christmas and New Year's Day is the only time my siblings and I all get along with little to no fighting. There's something about the cheery music and lights and gingerbread cookies that makes us want to spend time together.

Dream Elise experienced all of that for me, and I have no idea what I missed.

Why did this have to happen to me?

Cora turns into a driveway, and I follow, realizing we're here. Her house looks the same as always. As Cora walks up to her enclosed front porch, I immediately remember the rainy afternoons we used to spend there playing board games.

Once we're inside, Cora turns around to face me. "Want to go up to my room to talk?"

"Sure."

"Do you want a snack or drink first?" she asks as she takes off her shoes.

I slip mine off, too. "No, thanks."

"Mom, I'm home!" Cora says.

"Okay," I hear Cora's mom say from the kitchen down the hall.

"Elise Jackson is here, too," Cora says. "Her dad's coming to pick her up soon, so we'll be in my room."

"Elise?" Cora's mom comes out of the kitchen and gives a warm smile when she sees us. "Oh, Elise! It's so nice to see you. How's your mom?"

"She's good," I say. "She said she was going to reach out to you."

"I'll text her now. It's been too long."

"Let's go upstairs," Cora says.

I follow her up to her room and as soon as we walk in, something soft rubs against my leg.

"Poppy!" I say.

I crouch down to pet the orange tabby cat, who starts purring.

"I haven't seen you in forever," I say.

Cora's family adopted Poppy as a kitten when we were in kindergarten. They'd already had an older cat, a gray one named Milo.

"Is Milo around here somewhere?" I ask Cora.

She shakes her head. "No. He died a couple of years ago."

"I'm so sorry," I say.

"It's okay. He lived to be eighteen, so he had a long life," Cora says. "I'm trying to convince my parents to let us get another kitten, though."

"That would be cool," I agree.

As I stare around Cora's room, memories start flooding back. We spent a lot of time in here as little kids. Cora was always into bright colors, and her parents had put up a big rainbow wall decal above her bed. It's still here. I always loved hanging out on Cora's daybed, which is covered in pillows and soft blankets. It looks like her stuffie collection has grown a lot. I recognize some of the other décor she had back then—a coin bank that's shaped like a red gummy bear, and a small lamp that's a white ceramic mouse holding a light bulb.

There are some new things in here, like a tall bookshelf filled with art supplies, and bins filled with paints and markers. There's one shelf of books so I walk over and peer at the titles. There are a few novels, but most of them are crafting books, including ones on crochet and hand lettering. Then I notice something in between them—a rectangular wooden box with a curved edge along the top.

"What's this?" I ask Cora.

"A book nook," she says. "I mean, it will be once I

finish it. I'm still trying to decide what the final design should be."

"What's a book nook?"

"It's like a diorama that you can put between the books on your shelf. It's meant to look like a tiny room or scene. I got this frame from the craft store, but now I need to paint it and design the inside. I'll show you some examples." Cora types something into her phone and hands it to me.

I scroll through the book nook images. They're all boxes between books on a shelf, but of different sizes and widths. One of them looks like the inside of a forest, with moss around the bottom, and mini trees and mushrooms along the sides. Another looks like a little library scene, with a bookshelf of tiny books on the back wall, a small rug, a lounge chair, and a teeny side table with a teacup and saucer. There are even fairy lights strung around the perimeter of that one.

"These are so cute!"

"I know, right?" Cora says.

"How are you going to decorate yours?" I ask.

"I might re-create downtown. I can have the road going through the middle, and a few of my favorite shops on either side, with their awnings and signs. But I'm still brainstorming."

"That sounds fun."

Cora's always been creative. When we were little, I'd draw pictures with markers while she'd take it a step further and create elaborate collages out of bits of paper and leaves. She doesn't seem to just dream about pretty things—she turns them into reality using whatever materials she can. It's pretty cool.

"Wait, is this a speaker?" I pick up a small object that's shaped like a bunny. "It's so cute. Where'd you get it?"

"Oh, that?" Cora says, looking at it carefully. "Wow, I forgot I even had that. It was . . . a Christmas gift."

She sits on her bed next to Poppy. "Anyway, what did you want to talk to me about?"

"Oh, yeah." Dad will be here soon, so I better get to it. I take a seat on the other side of her bed. "I'm just going to spit it out, and I'm warning you—you might think I'm crazy or something."

"I won't think you're crazy," Cora says.

"Just wait." I take a deep breath, and then say, "I think . . . I . . . jumped ahead . . . in . . . time."

There. I said it. I stare at Cora's tie-dye comforter and brace myself for her reaction. When she doesn't immediately respond, I wish I could take back what I just said.

Finally, Cora asks, "What do you mean, jumped ahead?" When I glance up at her, she seems intrigued.

I exhale. "Last October, the night of the fall carnival—remember? I saw you there. That night, Melinda and Ivy slept over at my house, and we all went to bed in sleeping bags in my basement. But then when I woke up the next day, it wasn't October anymore. It was a week ago. April eighth. At first, I thought I lost my memory, and maybe that's still what happened, but I honestly don't think so."

"So, you think you, like, time traveled?" Cora asks.

I'm grateful that when she asks that, she doesn't sound judgmental, only curious.

"Maybe? But I'm not sure about that because to my parents and siblings, and it seems like to Melinda and Ivy, I was here the whole time. To you, too, right? I've been here the whole time?"

Cora seems surprised at the question, but then nods. "Yeah. I think so."

"Exactly. If I'd time traveled, then why was there a version of myself still going through my life? Amnesia makes more sense, like my brain blocked out six months of time. I don't know how else to explain it, but in my gut, I know it's not amnesia. I know this isn't a medical thing. I have this feeling that it's . . ." I pause and shake my head.

Cora leans closer to me. "That it's what?"

"This is going to sound nuts, but maybe something . . .

*magical* . . . happened to me. Something . . . paranormal. Oh my gosh, I can't believe I just said that out loud." I put my head in my hands and brace myself for Cora's laugh.

"Maybe it did."

I look up at Cora. "What?"

"Maybe something magical or paranormal did happen to you."

She looks totally serious, and a weight lifts off my chest.

"You believe me?"

She nods. "Actually, I . . ." Then she pauses.

"You what?" I ask.

"I've always kind of believed in magic," Cora finally says. "I mean, beyond the tooth fairy and stuff. I don't know. Strange things happen sometimes. Just because something hasn't been proven yet doesn't mean it's not possible."

"I'm so glad you believe me." My instinct was right. Cora must like Daphne's Delights because she believes that magic is possible.

And I guess I believe it now, too.

"What are you going to do now?" Cora asks.

"I want to figure out what happened to me during the time I missed," I say. "I still don't know why I'm not friends with Ivy and Melinda anymore. And, honestly,

I'm not sure how *we* got to be friends again. You and me. Can you tell me?"

"How we became friends again?" Cora repeats.

"Yeah. Do you know what happened with me, Ivy, and Melinda? And when or how the two of us started hanging out?"

"I'm not sure about Ivy and Melinda," Cora says. "As for us, you came to photography club one day. We became friends again there."

"Really? I wonder what made me go to photography club. . . . I don't usually take a lot of pictures."

"Maybe Mr. G invited you? He can be very convincing."

I sigh. "I hate that I don't know for sure. I want to know what happened to me, what caused this. What if it happens again?"

Cora looks at me like she doesn't know how to answer that.

"At the very least, I want to know exactly what happened in the time I lost," I say. "There has to be a way for me to piece it all together."

"I can help you, if you want."

"Yeah?"

"Sure. You're my friend, even if you don't remember how it happened." She laughs.

"Right . . . Thanks. I'd love your help."

Cora smiles, and I do, too.

Right then, her mom calls for us. "Elise's dad is here," she adds.

When we get downstairs, Dad is by the front door talking to Cora's mom.

"Want to come over after school tomorrow?" I ask Cora, and then look at our parents. "If it's okay."

"It's fine with me," Dad says.

"Me, too," Cora's mom says. "I love that you two have reconnected."

Cora and I smile at each other.

I still don't have answers, but at least I won't have to figure this out alone.

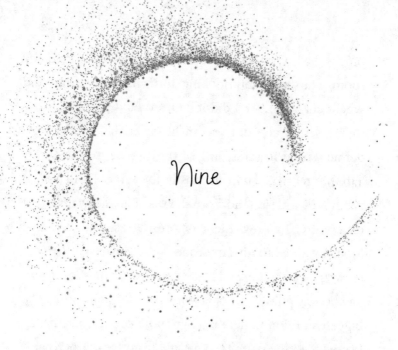

# Nine

*How do I begin to* piece together everything that happened to me during six whole months? It feels too overwhelming, so I decide to focus on the two main questions I'm desperate to answer:

1. Why, and when, did Ivy and Melinda stop talking to me?

2. How did this time jump—or whatever this is— happen to me?

Cora comes to my house the next day after school, and we bring snacks up to my room—peanut butter crackers, a bowl of grapes, and cups of strawberry lemonade.

We put everything on my desk and then I flop down

on my bed. Cora sits next to me and peers around my room. She's probably looking for what's the same and what's changed, like I did in her room.

The last time Cora was in here was before the pandemic started in the spring of third grade, so four years ago. My room is laid out mostly the same. I still have a twin bed, a desk, and bookshelves. But the walls are a different color now. Right before middle school, I told Mom I wanted to give my room a makeover. We painted the walls navy blue, and I also got a new white comforter and accent pillows in blue with pops of light pink. The biggest addition in here is a light pink cozy armchair that I convinced my parents to get me from Ikea. It's the perfect reading chair.

"I like what you did with the place," Cora says.

"Thanks."

Cora's wearing her locket over her T-shirt. I haven't worn mine since the day I went to Daphne's Delights, so I grab it from my jewelry box and put it on.

"Now we match," I say.

Cora glances at the locket around my neck and beams.

"So . . . what's the plan?" she asks.

"I want to find out what happened with Ivy and Melinda first. I need to know why they suddenly hate me." I grab a couple of grapes and pop them into my mouth. While I chew, I think. How can I get the full story if Melinda and Ivy won't talk to me?

"I wish my parents would let me have social media," I say after a minute. "They won't let me join any of the apps until I'm in high school."

Dad, who has a job in tech, locked my phone down so I can only make calls or text people on it. It was the same with Shay and Theo when they were my age.

"Ivy has an account on Booster," I add. "She's always posting pictures and videos. For all I know, she posted about what happened between us. Maybe I can ask one of my siblings to borrow their phone."

But I already know they'll say no.

"You can use my phone," Cora says. "I'm barely ever on it, so my parents don't restrict anything. I don't have a Booster account, but we can create one if you want."

"Really?" I ask.

Cora shrugs. "Sure."

"Oh my gosh, thank you!"

"No problem." I watch as Cora unlocks her phone and downloads the Booster app. Then she creates an account under the username Corab823.

After that's done, she hands me the phone, and I type Ivy's username into the search bar: EyeVee215. But her account doesn't show up, even though I'm positive that's her username since I've looked at the app on her phone so many times. The numbers are for her birthday, February 15. I try searching for her full name, Ivy Yang. I scroll partway down the list, but none of the profile pictures look like her.

"Did she change her username?" I think out loud. I try searching for other variations of her name and original username, like EyeVeeY, IvyYang215, and Ivy215. She doesn't show up.

"Can you search by her phone number or email address instead?" Cora asks.

"Maybe." I poke around the app some more and find something. "Look, it's asking to search for your contacts. Do you have Ivy's number saved in your phone?"

Cora narrows her eyes at me, and my face warms.

"Sorry. I forgot you're not friends with her. I'll add it and we'll see what happens." I go into Cora's contacts and create a new one for Ivy. I check my phone to confirm Ivy's phone number and email address, and type those in, too, just in case. Then I close out the app and reopen it, so it refreshes.

When the message pops up asking to connect to Cora's contacts, I click on "continue" and give it permission. A list of usernames appears, and I scroll through it, looking for Ivy.

"I found her!" I say, relieved. I recognize her profile pic first, and then read the username next to it: DancerIvy215. That wasn't her username before. She must've changed it at some point. Maybe after she stopped talking to me.

Either way, I'm glad the contacts trick worked.

"Great." Cora scoots closer to me so she can see her phone screen, too.

But then I realize I have another problem. Ivy's account is private. Of course it is. Her parents aren't as strict as mine when it comes to her phone and apps, but they probably make sure all her accounts are private so no random people can see her pictures and videos.

"I can't see any of her stuff unless I follow her," I say. "I mean, unless *you* follow her."

"Okay . . . ," Cora says. "You can try following her under my account."

"Maybe we should fill in the rest of your profile first. So, it doesn't seem so random."

Cora nods.

"Do you have a picture that we can use for your profile pic?" I ask.

"I don't think so." Cora grabs the phone from me and looks through her photos. "I usually take pictures of my crafts or stuff for photography club. I'm not really into selfies."

"Can I take a picture of you now, so we can use that?"

"Okay." She shifts on my bed, like she's getting ready to pose.

"Maybe we should take it outside, where the lighting is better." Also, where it's not so obvious she's in my room. Ivy might recognize it in the background of Cora's pic and decide not to accept her as a follower. This already feels like a long shot.

We go outside and I position her in front of a tree. Cora smiles and I take a few close-up shots. Then she makes a silly face by sticking her tongue out and crossing her eyes. I snap a few of those as well.

"Think we can use the silly face one?" Cora asks with a laugh when I show her the photos.

"Not if we want Ivy to accept you," I say, and then realize how harsh that sounds.

Cora doesn't seem to notice. "I know, I was just joking."

We go back inside and add one of the first photos to her account.

"What do you want your profile to say?" I ask.

Cora shrugs. "I dunno."

"I guess we can just put your name. So, Ivy knows it's you."

"Okay."

I type in Cora's name and save it. I'm worried that Ivy won't accept Cora's follow request, since it's true that they aren't friends. But it's still worth trying.

I find Ivy's account again and click on the "request to follow" button.

"Now, we wait," I say.

"Now, we wait," Cora repeats.

I take a sip of lemonade and grab a handful of peanut butter crackers.

Meanwhile, Cora goes over to my bookshelves and starts looking at the titles. "You still read a ton, huh?"

"Yup."

"That's cool. Have you read all of these?"

My bookshelf can probably hold one hundred books, and right now it's three-quarters full. "All of them except the few that Dream Elise bought."

"Dream Elise?" Cora asks, confused.

"Oh. Uh." I pause. I definitely did not mean to say that out loud. "It sounds silly but it's what I've called the . . . version of myself, I guess . . . from the time I lost. Since it feels like that version of me was in a dream—or maybe, a nightmare—that I can't remember."

Cora nods like that makes total sense.

"I noticed she . . . I mean, that version of me . . . bought books." Then I say, "Hey, maybe when you finish making your own book nook, you can make one for me."

Cora looks over at me and grins. "I'd love to."

"Can I ask you something about photography club?" I say.

"Sure."

"What do we do with the photos we take? And how do we usually take them—on our phones? My phone has no pictures on them, which is weird. I checked the cloud, and all my pictures from before the time jump or whatever are there, but I don't see any from the last six months. It's like Dream Elise barely used my phone."

"For photography club, sometimes kids use their own cameras or phones, but Mr. G also has a couple of nicer cameras that he lends out to students," Cora says. "Your parents have to sign a waiver to take it home for a couple days. Whatever pics you take on that are usually saved online under your school account."

My eyes light up. "I should check that account, then." I grab my laptop and log into my school email, then click on the files folder. I scan the page until I see a folder named Photography Club. I open it and see a bunch of photo files. "You were right!"

I start opening the photos, and quickly realize that they're all of Sunny's Books. Of course, since that's what my photo essay is about. I didn't use the camera to capture anything else.

"It's a dead end." I can't keep the disappointment out of my voice. I close my laptop and flop back onto my bed.

"Uh, Elise?" Cora says. Her back is facing me, but she twists around to look my way.

"Yeah?"

"Ivy accepted my follow request." She holds her phone out. "We can see everything now."

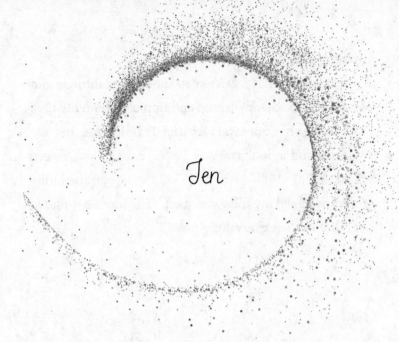

# Ten

*I learn two helpful things* from Ivy's Booster account:

1. Dream Elise *did* spend Halloween with Ivy and Melinda, and it looks like we dressed up as the witches from the Hocus Pocus movies. I was dressed as Mary, Ivy was Sarah, and Melinda was Winifred. From Ivy's photos, it looks like Dream Elise had a great time. I love that for her, while also hating that I don't remember any of it.

2. It seems like my friendship with the girls ended between Thanksgiving and Christmas break. That's when any photos with me in them stop. Unfortunately, Ivy didn't post about *why* she stopped talking to me. I just disappear from the photos in her feed just like I've

been erased from her life.

Even though this clearly happened months ago, it hurts like it just happened. What did I do to deserve this?

At least now I have a time frame.

On a Post-it note, I write, "What happened between Thanksgiving and Christmas???" and stick it to the bulletin board above my desk.

"Thanks for your help," I tell Cora when it's time for her to go home.

Our moms are in the middle of a conversation when we get downstairs.

"Anytime," Cora says. "Lunch tomorrow?"

"Sure."

Our moms smile at each other. Mom's always liked Cora so I know she's excited we're friends again. I'm happy about it, too, and grateful that she's helping me solve this huge mystery. But I still miss Ivy and Melinda. If I can get my friendship with them back, maybe Cora can join our group.

Back in my room, I try to think of other ways to find out what happened between October and April. Then I remember that my parents always take a lot of photos of my siblings and me. Enough to make us sometimes beg them to put their phones away so we can stop posing for pics.

I go downstairs and ask Mom if I can look at the photos on her phone so I can message some to myself, and she agrees. I scroll back to October's pictures and find the ones of Ivy, Melinda, and me that Mom took the night of the sleepover. She'd snapped a pic of the three of us sitting on our sleeping bags, grinning with our arms slung around each other. As I scroll through the photos after that, I see all these pictures of myself that I don't remember her taking. I zoom in on my face in one picture from when my parents, siblings, and I put up and decorated our Christmas tree. We always do it the weekend after Thanksgiving. I look just like myself, except I'm wearing sweats I don't recognize.

Mom took a few videos, too, so I watch one of them. It's weird to see myself moving around, hanging ornaments, laughing, and singing along to Christmas music, and know it's not me. Or at least it doesn't feel like me since this version of me wasn't there. That's Dream Elise.

I open up one video clip of me, Shay, and Theo doing some kind of trending dance in front of Shay's phone. She sometimes does video trends on Booster, but it'd been a while since she asked me and Theo to do one with her. The song is "All I Want for Christmas Is You" but sped up so Mariah Carey's voice sounds like a chipmunk.

Theo comes into the kitchen to get an iced tea from

the fridge when I'm in the middle of watching it.

"Oh god, is that song trending again?" he asks. "It was in my head for *weeks*."

"I don't know," I say. "I'm just watching a video from December." I show him Mom's phone screen.

"Oh yeah. That was fun, even if the song made me want to claw my eyeballs out."

Maybe I'd agree with him . . . if I could remember.

Theo leaves the kitchen, and I scroll some more, but in the end, none of Mom's pictures or videos explain what happened to me. They just remind me of what I lost—not just my friends, but these moments in my life.

Moments that I might never get back.


The next day, I keep thinking of ways to uncover what happened between October and April. I can try talking to other people that Melinda and Ivy are friendly with, but I'm not sure how to ask about something I should already know about. I also don't want Ivy and Melinda to find out that I've been asking about them.

Then I remember TJ Patel and Harrison Gibbs, the two kids that usually sit on the other side of the cafeteria table where Melinda, Ivy, and I usually sit. The tables are shaped as an octagon, so a lot of times two different groups will share them during lunch. Since the table's not *that* big, maybe they overheard the girls talking about me.

I don't want to talk to them in the cafeteria, since Melinda and Ivy will be there.

Luckily, I have afternoon PE with Harrison. And when I tell Cora about my plan during lunch, she tells me that she has English with TJ.

"Will you talk to him?" I ask.

Cora bites her lip. "I don't know if I can."

"Why not?"

"I've never talked to TJ before," she says. "It'll be weird if I go up to him to ask him about this. I'll feel weird."

I can tell Cora's uncomfortable, by the way she's pulling at her twists. "It'll be a really quick conversation," I say to assure her.

"It's just . . . ," Cora says, her voice softening, "I get anxious sometimes."

"Oh." I wasn't expecting that. Though, now that I think about it, maybe that's why she seems to keep to herself around school. "You have anxiety?"

Cora nods. "Not all the time. And not with everyone. I don't mind talking to adults. Or you—since you've known me forever. But when talking to other kids . . . sometimes." Then she says, "But, if this is that important to you, I'll try."

"Really?" I ask. "I mean, you don't have to."

"No, I'll do it. It'll be good for me to face my fear."

"Thank you! You're the best."

Cora's mouth turns up in a smile.

In the gym, I'm supposed to be paying attention to our teacher as she explains the rules of the volleyball game we're about to play. Instead, I stand close to Harrison and whisper, "Hey." When he glances at me, I say, "Can I ask you something?"

"Me?" Harrison asks, forgetting to whisper back. The kids closest to us give him a funny look and his cheeks get red.

I wait a beat for everyone to turn back to our teacher, and then whisper, "Yeah."

I've never really talked to Harrison before, so it makes sense that he's surprised I'm doing it now. We sometimes said a quick "hi" or flashed a friendly smile when we were the first ones at our lunch table, but once our own friends showed up, we went back to ignoring each other.

I don't know how much time I have, so I talk fast. "It's about Melinda and Ivy. I know you're not friends with them, but since you sit on the other side of our . . . I mean, their . . . lunch table . . . have you heard them say anything about me?"

"What do you mean?" he asks, finally getting the hint and whispering.

Our teacher is starting to break us into groups, so I get to the point.

"They stopped being friends with me," I say. "And I still don't know what happened. Have you ever overheard them talk about me at our table in the cafeteria?"

Harrison's eyes light up, like he finally understands what I'm talking about.

*He knows something!* There's a flutter of excitement in my chest.

But then Harrison says, "You're not friends with them anymore?"

*Seriously?* "You didn't notice? I haven't sat at their table in . . ." I still don't know exactly how long. "A while."

"Sorry," Harrison says. "I didn't notice. But honestly, I don't notice stuff like that. When TJ got braces, it took me weeks to realize. And I was talking to him *a lot* during those weeks. My mom says I need to be more observant."

*Clearly.* "Okay. Thanks anyway."

After school, I meet Cora at her locker.

"How did it go in English class?" I ask. "Were you able to talk to TJ?"

Cora grins. "Yes! I was so nervous all throughout class. I was sweating so bad. But when the bell rang, I went up to him before I could change my mind. I tapped him on the shoulder and asked if I could ask him a question."

"And?"

"Thankfully, he was really nice," Cora says, relieved. "And he said you stopped sitting with Ivy and Melinda after we got back from winter break. If they talked about you in the cafeteria, it was too low for him to overhear."

My heart sinks. "Okay," I say. "That narrows it down some more, at least. Whatever happened, it must've been during winter break.

"I'm proud of you," I tell Cora. "For facing your fear."

"Thanks," Cora says. "I'm proud of me, too. By the way, do you want to get together this weekend to take pictures? So you have new ones to show Mr. G on Monday? I'm borrowing his fancy camera for the weekend so I can show you how to use it."

"Actually . . . I've been thinking of quitting photography club," I say.

"What?" Cora asks. "Why?"

"I know nothing about photography," I say with a shrug. "Maybe it was Dream Elise's thing, but it's not mine. What's the point of staying in the club now?"

"Because it's fun! I can show you what you need to know if we meet up this weekend, so you don't feel out of place anymore. I promise you'll enjoy it."

"I don't know . . ." I can't help but feel depressed about everything. The lack of answers. This lost feeling. I was looking forward to holing up in my room and reading books again all weekend.

"Just meet with me on Saturday to take some pictures, and then you can decide," Cora says. "If you still aren't into it on Monday, you can tell Mr. G you're quitting."

I was planning to simply stop coming to photography club and try my best to avoid Mr. G in the hallways. But I guess the right thing to do would be to let him know I wasn't coming back. The thought makes me shudder.

"Deal?" Cora asks.

Meeting up with Cora could be a nice distraction from everything that's been going on. And since she's my only friend right now, it would be nice to get to know her again. Plus, she just went way out of her comfort zone to talk to TJ for me. So, I can do this for her.

"Fine," I say. "I'll come."

"Yay!" Cora says.

I smile. At least someone is excited to spend time with me.

"Let's meet at Sunny's Books," I say. "I haven't been back inside since the time jump, so maybe it'll spark a memory. Plus, it's my happy place."

Cora grins. "Sounds like a plan."

# Eleven

Sunny's Books has always felt like my second home. It's so familiar, down to the smell of old wooden shelves and new book pages. I'm glad the store still smells the same. When I walk in, I spot Sunny lying on the ground in a patch of light streaming in from the front window. She doesn't get up when she sees me, but her tail starts wagging. I lean down to pet the top of her head and rub her chin. My parents won't let us get a dog, so I love to get as many cuddles as possible when I'm here. Sunny licks my hand, and I wonder if she recognizes that this is the *real* me, not Dream Elise. Lots of people believe dogs can sense the supernatural.

I realize that a bunch of new books have come out since the last time I remember being here. That's six months of new releases! I'm about to head back to the middle grade fantasy section to check them out when I spot Cora.

She's standing next to one of the front tables, looking at a book. The display sign says, "Spring into Reading." Half the table has cookbooks and gardening books, and the other half has novels with pastel or floral covers.

When I walk up to her, Cora is flipping through a photography book showing botanical gardens around the world.

"Hey," I say.

"Oh, hey," she says, and looks back down at the book. "Look how beautiful these pictures are. Dahlias are my favorite flower. When my cousin got married last summer, her bouquet and centerpieces had a lot of dahlias, and I took so many pictures of them."

"They are really pretty," I say. "So, you're really into photography, then?"

Cora closes the book and puts it back into place on the table. "It's my current fixation. When I get into a hobby, I go hard."

"What other hobbies have you had?"

"I got really into crocheting animals for a while. And

then modern calligraphy. Once I start my book nook, I'm sure that'll become my next obsession."

"Wow," I say.

"Anyway, let's take some pictures!" Cora says.

"Okay . . . where should I start?"

Cora thinks for a second, and then asks, "Why do you love this bookstore so much?"

"Books are my fixation, except I never get tired of them," I tell her. "Reading's my escape."

"Well, you can get books anywhere. Why this bookstore?"

I glance around and spot Beth at the register checking someone out. She sees me and flashes a smile before returning her attention to the customer.

"This bookstore's special. Beth, the owner, really cares about helping customers find the perfect book."

Beth has an amazing memory, and always remembers what kinds of books you like, and what she's already recommended to you in the past. So, when you come in looking for something new, she knows exactly what book to hand you. She's magic like that.

"Same with the other booksellers here. Everyone's always so nice and helpful. And of course, there's Sunny, who just lights up the store," I add.

Cora's grinning at me. "I love that. Since Sunny's lying

in that sunny spot, you should get a picture of her with the light framing her."

I stare at Cora blankly. "I have no idea how to do that."

"I'll show you." She reaches into the small black bag that I'm only now noticing she's been carrying this whole time, and takes out a camera.

"Is that's Mr. G's camera?" I ask.

"Yup. It's so cool that he lets us borrow it. We just have to be *really* careful." She puts the camera strap around her neck and walks over to where Sunny is lying on her side.

I follow.

"Hi, pup pup," Cora says to Sunny, like she's talking to a baby. "What a sweet girl." She rubs Sunny's belly. "Let's try to get a picture of you, okay?"

Cora puts the camera to her face and moves around Sunny, looking for the best angle. She practically lies down next to Sunny so she's in line with the dog's face. "This could be good." Cora adjusts the lens by twisting it. "A close-up of Sunny's face, but with the light and bookshelf behind her. Here—take a look."

I wait for Cora to stand up but then I realize she wants me to get on the floor next to her so she can show me the angle. After looking around the store to make sure nobody's staring at us, I get down on the ground.

Cora holds out the camera and I look in the viewfinder.

It's a good thing Sunny is a chill older dog, because she stays still, staring at the camera with a curious expression. I see what Cora means. The sun is shining in through the window on one side of Sunny, and behind her, the bookshelf is blurred.

"Click this button when you're ready." She points to the one she means. "You should take a bunch, and we'll see which one comes out the best."

I make sure Sunny's centered in the shot and click the button a few times. Even though the camera looks really complicated to use, this part is easy. When I'm done, I lower the camera from my face and stand up.

"Let's see how they came out," Cora says as she takes the camera from me. She presses some buttons, and the latest pictures appear on the little screen.

"They look awesome!" Cora says as she scrolls through them.

"They do look good," I agree. Cora's vision totally worked. Sunny looks adorable. I'll have to send this picture to Beth.

"Admit it. That was fun, right?" Cora says.

I smile. "Yeah. It was."

"Want to get some pictures of the outside of the store?" Cora asks.

"Okay."

Outside, Cora teaches me some more about how to use the camera. I take some shots of the storefront from different angles. I also get some of Main Street, and the flowers hanging from the streetlight posts.

I don't normally take a lot of scenery pictures—usually just selfies of myself or with friends. It's nice to see the bookstore and this neighborhood literally through a different lens.

"I told you this would be fun," Cora says.

"Yeah." I grin at her. "It really is."

Cora raises her eyebrows. "Does that mean you'll stay in photography club?"

"I guess," I say.

"Yay!" Cora says.

When we're done taking photos of the bookstore, I give the fancy camera back to Cora and ask to see her phone. "Now that you taught me how to do serious photography, I'm going to teach you how to get a good selfie."

Cora laughs. "Okay."

I stand right next to her so our arms touch, and we lean our heads closer together. With her phone in my right hand, I stretch it out and a little toward the sky.

"Look at that green dot in the corner of the screen, where the lens is, and smile." We both grin into the camera, and I click the photo button a few times.

When we're done, I show her the results. "It's not perfect, but it's . . . us. If you know what I mean."

"I love it," Cora says.

Cora and I have some extra time before our parents pick us up. We decide to walk over and grab drinks from the bubble tea shop, which Cora says is her favorite.

"I've been thinking about who else I should talk to about Ivy and Melinda, to find out what happened," I say once we have our drinks and are seated at a table outside.

"Why don't you just ask one of them?" Cora says.

"I thought of that. But won't it be weird for me to admit that I don't remember what happened between us? I don't want anyone else to know about the time jump. And I don't want Ivy and Melinda to think I'm nuts."

"Who cares what they think about you?"

"I care."

"But why?" Cora asks. "Isn't it obvious that you don't matter to them anymore?"

Her words sting. But I can't argue since she's right.

"I *used* to matter to them," I say. "Before the time jump."

"Right, but that was before." Cora looks at me like she doesn't get it.

"You remember Amelia Davis?" I ask. "She used to go

95

to our school but moved last year?"

"Of course," Cora says.

"We became really good friends during the fourth grade, when everything was still weird because of the pandemic. But then last year, her mom, who's a surgeon, got a job at a different hospital, and so they had to move. All the way across the country. I felt so down when she left. Like I was lost. I didn't want to do anything except stay in my room and read books so I could forget about real life.

"But then I got lucky. I met Ivy and Melinda and clicked with them. They started asking me to hang out with them more—to watch movies or walk around downtown. We went to the end-of-school-year dance together and had so much fun. Suddenly, I was part of this trio, and I was happy again. Last summer was amazing."

I think of one time when Ivy, Melinda, and I came to this bubble tea shop. We each got drinks, and then decided to walk to the beach. It only takes five minutes to drive from downtown to the beach. But of course, walking takes longer. It was fine at first, but it was so hot and humid and sunny that by the time we got to the beach thirty minutes later, we were so sweaty, and our bubble tea was long gone.

So, the first thing we did was kick off our shoes and

run into the water. We didn't have bathing suits on, so we stopped when the cool water hit just below our shorts. It felt amazing.

After walking along the shore for a while, we dried off in the sun. Then we went to the playground next to the beach and swung on the swings. By the time our parents picked us up a while later, we were sticky, sandy, and possibly sunburned, but we were also happy.

"So yeah," I say to Cora now. "I want them back. They meant a lot to me. They still do. And unlike Amelia, they're still here. Whatever Dream Elise did to ruin our friendship, I want to fix it. Because that *wasn't* me."

Cora sighs and says, "All right."

She doesn't understand because she doesn't know Ivy and Melinda like I do.

I stare out into the street, at the cars driving by and people walking with shopping bags. "There has to be someone I can talk to about what happened with us. Besides Ivy and Melinda. They must've told *someone*."

Just then, my cell phone ringtone blares, making us both jump.

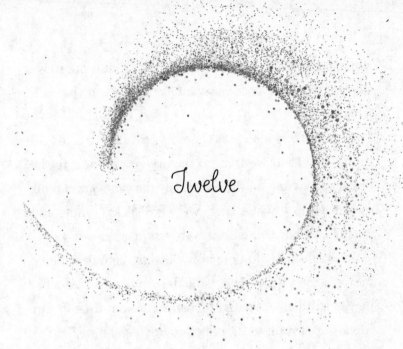

# Twelve

Amelia's name is on my phone screen.

Amelia—my old best friend who moved away a year ago. Who I was just talking about. Who I haven't spoken to in . . . well, since the middle of last summer.

When she first moved away, we video called each other all the time. She'd show me how she was setting up her new room and talk about her new town. Amelia's really into graphic novels and comics, and apparently there's a good comic store near her new house.

I'd tell her the latest gossip about kids from school. Amelia loves hearing gossip. But then she made new friends at summer camp, and I started hanging out more with Ivy and Melinda. After a while, we video chatted less and less, until we basically stopped.

Until now.

I answer the call after the third ring.

The first thing I notice when Amelia appears on-screen is her shorter brown hair. It used to be super long, falling halfway down her back. We used to joke that if she kept letting it grow, she'd eventually be able to sit on it. But now it's barely shoulder-length. When did she cut it?

"Hi!" I say. "How are you?"

Her familiar smile lights up the screen and warms my heart. "I'm good," she says. Then, "Why do you sound so surprised? It was your turn to call me. Did you forget?"

I was supposed to call her? Since when?

Amelia is waiting for me to answer, so I make something up. "Yeah, sorry. I . . . got distracted."

"Oh okay," she says, like it's no big deal. "Where are you, anyway?"

"The bubble tea shop downtown." I move the phone so she can see the shop behind me. "I'm here with my friend Cora."

"Photography club Cora?"

"You know about photography club?"

"Of course!" Amelia gives me a funny look. "What's going on with you? You're acting weird."

"Sorry. It's nothing." I pause. "Remind me why I was calling you again?"

"Because I called you last month, and we said we'd alternate."

"Right . . ."

I piece together what Amelia is saying. We talked last month? And maybe even the month before? I wonder how long it's been since we reconnected—and how. I know it happened during my lost time. Did she reach out to me, or did I reach out to her? It's weird to know that Amelia was actually talking to Dream Elise. I guess she couldn't tell the difference.

"Is it not a good time?" Amelia asks. "We can talk later instead. I was just bored so I thought I'd call."

Out of the corner of my eye, I see Cora waving her hand at me from across the table.

"Can you hold on for one second?" I ask Amelia.

"Sure."

I mute the call and turn off the camera. "What?" I ask in a low voice even though I know Amelia can't hear me.

"I thought of something," Cora says. "Maybe Amelia knows what happened between you, Melinda, and Ivy. Since it sounds like your . . . time jump self . . . talked to her recently."

My eyes light up. "Maybe. But how would I ask her

without her thinking something's up? I don't want to tell her about the time jump. It's enough that you know about it for now."

Then an idea pops into my head. "You could ask her," I tell Cora.

"What? Me?"

"Yes. You can tell her that you don't know the full story . . . and I won't tell you. Because I'm tired of talking about it. Trust me. Amelia loves to gossip. If I tell her that it's okay to tell you, she will."

Cora frowns. "I don't know . . ."

"I know you get anxious, but I promise that Amelia is super nice," I say. "And I'll be right here. Though it might be better if I pretend to leave the table . . ."

Cora still looks unsure.

"I'll set it up. Tell her it's my idea." I look down at the phone to make sure Amelia's still there. I don't want to keep her waiting too long. "Please? You're the only one who can help me."

Cora exhales. "Okay. I'll do it."

"Thank you!"

I turn the camera back on and unmute myself. "I'm back. And actually, can you do me a favor?"

"What kind of favor?" Amelia asks.

"Cora keeps asking me what happened with Melinda

and Ivy—why we're not friends anymore—but I honestly don't want to talk about it. It's too . . . painful."

Amelia nods sympathetically.

"Do you think you can tell her?" Then I add, "You'll be doing me a favor. Then Cora can stop asking me about it and I can go back to pretending it never happened."

Technically, I don't know if Amelia knows what happened. But if we've been talking again for months, the odds are she does. I hold my breath while I wait for her to respond.

"Sure, if you want," Amelia says.

Yes! Amelia knows what happened! I stop myself from smiling so she doesn't get suspicious.

"Thank you! I'm going to give her my phone and go inside to use the bathroom. You can talk while I'm gone."

"Okay," Amelia says.

I stand up but instead of going to the bathroom, I pick up my chair and gently place it closer to Cora so I can see the screen, but Amelia can't see me.

"Hey," Cora says.

"Hey," Amelia says.

My heart feels like it's about to explode as I wait for Amelia to start talking.

"Okay, so apparently it started over winter break," Amelia explains, now looking giddy at the chance to share this piece of gossip. "Elise told me that she was hanging out with Ivy one day when Melinda wasn't around. That was happening more and more, because Melinda got a couple of bad grades, so her parents weren't letting her hang out with her friends as much.

"But then when they all got back to school, this rumor about Ivy started going around. Something about Ivy stuffing her bra with tissues. Everyone was talking about it, and at some point, the principal had to tell everyone over the loudspeaker that it was inappropriate to talk about another classmate's body. I guess everyone knew the principal was talking about Ivy."

*That's so embarrassing*, I think. *Poor Ivy.*

"That was bad enough," Amelia continued. "But *then*, Ivy told Elise that she found out that *she* was the one who started the rumor."

I gasp and then immediately cover my mouth, hoping Amelia didn't hear it.

"Ivy thought *Elise* started the rumor?" Cora repeats.

"Yup," Amelia says. "I'm surprised you didn't hear about it."

Wait. Why *hadn't* Cora heard about it if everyone else was talking about it?

"I'm the last person to hear rumors, if I hear them at all," Cora says.

I guess that explains why TJ and Harrison didn't know about it either. They don't seem like the gossiping type.

"What happened next?" Cora asks.

"Melinda took Ivy's side," Amelia says. "So, first Elise was sad about that. That's how we started video chatting again. She called me out of nowhere, crying."

Wow, so I reached out to Amelia after that all happened. Or Dream Elise did.

"That's not the worst part, though," Amelia says.

"There's more?" Cora asks exactly what I'm thinking.

"Yup. Elise got Melinda to admit that *she* was the one who made up the story about Ivy! She found out Melinda told everyone that Elise started it."

I almost gasp again.

"What?" Cora squeals. "Why would she do that?"

"Because she was jealous of how close Elise and Ivy were getting, just the two of them," Amelia says. "Like, they had their own inside jokes and stuff. So, this was her way to get Elise out of the picture."

I slump down in my chair in disbelief. How could Melinda do this to me? My mind races as I try to process what I just learned.

Cora and Amelia keep talking but their voices feel far away.

"Did Ivy find out that Melinda made all of it up?" Cora asks.

"Elise tried to tell her, but Ivy didn't believe her. She believed Melinda."

"Wow," Cora says.

"I know," Amelia agrees. "Terrible, right? So that's the story."

"Thanks for telling me," Cora says.

"No problem. Is Elise back yet?"

Cora pretends to look for me. "Yeah, she's coming back now. One sec."

I snap out of my daze when she puts her hand over mine.

"Elise?" Cora whispers.

I glance between her and my phone, which is facedown on the table. Even though I have no idea what to say to Amelia, I can't keep her hanging. I exhale and pick up the phone.

"Hey. So, uh, thanks for that." I barely choke out the words.

"Anytime!"

"Can we talk later?" I ask. "My dad's going to be here to pick me up in a minute."

"Definitely."

We say goodbye and I hang up the call.

I put my head down on the table.

"Are you okay?" Cora asks.

No. I'm not okay. Not only did Melinda reject me, sabotage my friendship with Ivy, and lie, but Ivy believed her.

I'm so stunned, I can't even cry.

All this time, I thought Ivy and Melinda had both genuinely liked me and were happy we were all friends. But I couldn't have been more wrong.

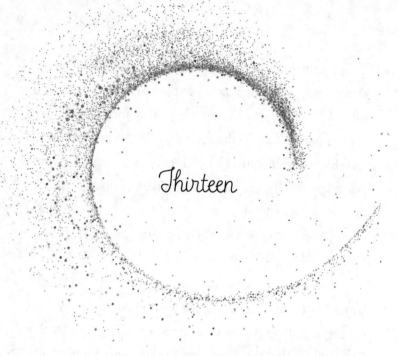

## Thirteen

*I finally know the truth,* but now I don't know what to do with it. How could Ivy believe that I'd make up a rumor about her? I thought she knew me better than that. And why would Melinda get jealous of Ivy and me hanging out without her? I would never try to make her feel left out, and I'm sure Ivy wouldn't either. She's always going out of her way to make other people happy.

I think back to how our friendship began. Melinda *was* a little standoffish in the beginning when we first hung out in Ivy's dance studio basement. But that didn't seem to last long.

Sometime after that, Melinda and I got into a conversation during lunch at school about sibling drama. She's one of five, and the middle child. She admitted that she sometimes feels overshadowed by her other siblings. I told her that I could kind of relate, since as the youngest in my family, I'm not always taken seriously. Ivy's an only child, so she just listened to Melinda and me talk. I remember feeling it was the first time that Melinda and I really bonded.

I also figured Melinda's family life was why she's sometimes sensitive when it came to me and Ivy. Like during the sleepover in October when she got upset that I already owned the book she'd gotten me. Even though it wasn't a big deal.

Still, I thought our friendship meant more to her.

Something must've happened during my lost time to lead to this. Something big that made Melinda want to do something this drastic.

My thoughts freeze.

Wait a minute. This has to be Dream Elise's fault. Dream Elise must've said or done the wrong thing at some point, and offended Melinda. Not that it excuses Melinda making up a terrible rumor about me and Ivy. But if I never jumped ahead in time, the real version of me would've been there during winter break and the months before. I could've prevented this.

Now that I know the truth, I need to find a way to go back to October, before all of this happened. First, I need to figure out what caused the time jump.

By the time I'm back in school on Monday, surrounded by all my classmates, I feel gross. Not only does Ivy think I started a nasty rumor about her, but other kids do, too. I don't want people thinking I'm that kind of person. I'm a *good* friend. I'm not perfect, but I always thought that my friends would come to me if there was a problem. Maybe Melinda *did* come to me first. Because that's the thing— besides what Amelia shared, I'm totally in the dark.

At the start of lunch period, I message Cora and tell her I'm spending lunch in the library. I want to be by myself for a while.

The next time I see her is that afternoon at photography club. I was going to skip it but realized that I wanted to see what Mr. G thinks of the pictures I took at Sunny's Books on Saturday. And I can talk to Cora about what I plan to do next.

Cora and I don't get to talk right away because Mr. G begins the meeting with announcements.

"First, we only have four more weeks until our photography showcase," Mr. G says with a grin. "Who's excited?"

"Woo!" someone says, and other kids snap their fingers in agreement.

"These weeks will go by quickly. So, as you continue to take photos for your essays, don't forget all the lessons I shared earlier in the year. I want to especially remind you to capture a variety of angles in your pictures. When you find something to photograph, take the obvious shot, but then move around and see what other perspectives there are. How else can you view that building or object? What can you get a close-up of?" Mr. G starts moving his body like he's taking a picture from different angles.

Then he picks up a few prints from his desk. "Here's an example. I shot this photo of the Golden Gate Bridge when I visited San Francisco last summer." He holds up a picture showing a wide shot of the bridge, with a beach and shoreline in front.

"Then I got creative with my angles." Mr. G holds up a picture that must've been taken on the bridge, because it's showing the same orange beams close-up from below. There's fog in the background, making the scene look eerie.

"I even got this," Mr. G says, holding up a picture showing the bridge from above.

"How'd you take that one?" a kid named Ryan asks. "Were you in a helicopter?"

"Yes, I went on a helicopter tour," Mr. G says. "But if

it was allowed, I would've used a drone. I have one that can hold one of my action cameras and fly over things."

"That's really cool," Ryan says.

"You don't need a helicopter or drone to get creative angles, though," Mr. G says. "Just think outside the box when you're taking your pictures, okay?"

We all nod.

"All right, keep working and I'll come around to take a look at your progress." He stops at a desk across the room.

"I uploaded all the photos from the weekend," Cora tells me. "I'll email you the ones you took."

"Thanks."

We grab computers from the cart at the front of the room and bring them back to our desks.

After I log into my school account, I open my email. When I see the photos from Cora, I save them to my drive. I start scrolling through them, saving the best ones that I want to show Mr. G into a separate folder.

"How are you feeling?" Cora asks. "Now that you know what happened."

"Not great," I admit.

"At least it's closure, right?" Cora says. "You saw their true colors and can move on."

"Not exactly," I say. "I don't want to move on. I want to fix this."

"What do you mean?" Cora asks.

"I want to figure out how to reverse the time jump, so I can get my friendship with Ivy and Melinda back."

"You *still* want to be friends with those girls?" Cora asks, shocked.

"Yeah." I lower my voice to a whisper. "I think this all has to do with the time jump. It wasn't even the real me that was there. It was Dream Elise."

"Wow," Cora says. "You know that was still you, right? More important, your so-called friends thought it was you and *still* dropped you."

*So-called* friends?

"Right," I say. "But how do I know that I was acting like myself? Maybe this happened because they thought I changed. Our friendship was solid back in October."

"Was it?" Cora asks, shaking her head at me.

"Yes!"

At least I thought it was. Is it so wrong that I want that back?

"Hi, girls," Mr. G says when he arrives at our desks. "Cora, do you have anything new to show me this week?"

"Yup," she says, and her annoyance from seconds ago disappears from her voice. "Yesterday was the play's dress rehearsal, so I got some really good shots from the audience."

"Great, let's see them," Mr. G says.

I try to focus on my own pictures while Mr. G and Cora talk, but I can't stop thinking about how I can get back to October. Something from the night of the fall carnival and sleepover must've caused this. What was off about that night? I can't think of anything.

"How about you, Elise?" Mr. G says. "Do you have any new photos?"

"I do, actually. Thanks to Cora's help." I smile at her, and she smiles back, but it seems a little forced.

First, I open the shot of Sunny on the ground with the sunbeam and bookshelf behind her.

"I love this one," Mr. G says. He genuinely sounds impressed. "This is exactly what I'm talking about. Way to get creative with the angle. I bet you had to get right on the ground to capture that."

"I did," I say, feeling proud.

"It's also a good example of my lesson from a few meetings ago on depth of field," Mr. G says. "Nice work."

I nod, even though I have no idea what that means. "Thanks!"

Mr. G looks through some of my other pictures and helps me choose a couple more to add to my photo essay collection.

Then he goes to the next set of students.

I watch Cora as she stares at a picture on her computer screen and uses a program to edit and enhance it. I can tell from the way her eyebrow is furrowed that she's still annoyed.

I don't want to lose Cora as a friend just because I want my other friends back. It's like what Mr. G has been talking about—you can see images from different angles and perspectives. Cora sees this whole situation differently from me.

"Hey, do you think you can show me how to edit photos," I ask Cora, "since you're so good at it?" I smile at her sweetly and hope she'll take the peace offering.

Cora looks at me and her expression softens. "Sure. Scoot over."

"Also . . . what's depth of field?" I ask sheepishly.

"Oh, that just means how much of the image is in focus."

"Got it," I say. "You're the best."

Cora smiles.

When photography club is over, Cora and I walk together to the front of school, where our parents will pick us up.

"I'm sorry I got so defensive before," I say.

"It's okay," Cora says.

I tried to put myself in her shoes. Now that we're

becoming friends again, she probably doesn't want it to end when I'm back with Ivy and Melinda. I don't want that either.

"I don't only want to get back to October because of what happened with Ivy and Melinda," I say. "I don't like that this happened to me, and I don't know how or why. And what if it happens again?"

"Another time jump?" Cora asks.

I shrug. "Who knows! That's why I want to solve this mystery. Will you help me? Please?"

Cora looks uneasy but finally says, "Okay."

"Great!" I hug her and she squeezes me back, tight. I forgot how good of a hugger she is. Melinda and Ivy always give half-hearted hugs.

I don't know if we'll find any clues, but I have a good idea of where to start.

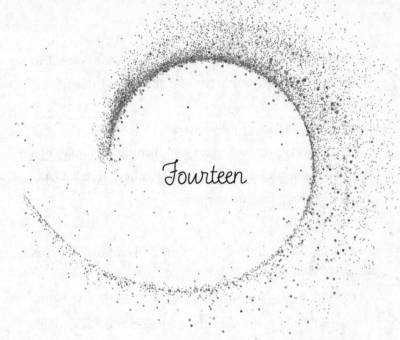

# Fourteen

"Back again, huh?" Ms. Harmon, the school librarian, says when I walk into the library during my lunch period the next day. "And you brought a friend. Hello, Cora."

"Hi, Ms. Harmon," Cora says.

"I don't mind if you two spend your lunch period in here, but only if you're still getting to eat something," Ms. Harmon says, her expression both friendly and concerned.

"Don't worry, we ate our lunches," I tell her. I quickly ate half my turkey sandwich at my locker and munched on some chips while I walked over here. Cora did the same with her wrap and carrot sticks.

Pretty much all of the library tables are empty, so we sit down at one closer to the back of the room so we can have some privacy.

"During my last class, I started writing down everything that happened that day in October," I tell Cora, showing her the page in my notebook.

That morning, I woke up and ate pancakes with my siblings. Then I ran errands with my mom to get everything we needed for the sleepover—drinks, snacks, and some decorations. That afternoon, Melinda and Ivy came over with their overnight stuff, and then we went to the carnival. At the sleepover, the only strange thing that happened was Mom bringing me the mysterious gift. . . .

"You were the one who dropped off the locket that night," I say to Cora. "My mom saw you on the camera but couldn't see your face."

"That was me," Cora says.

"Why didn't you ring the doorbell and give it to me yourself?"

Cora shrugs. "I was going to, but then I got nervous at the last second."

"Why?"

"I don't know. We hadn't really talked in a while."

"Why did you give me the locket, then?" I ask. "You

know I love it. I'm just wondering what made you buy me a gift in the first place."

"I guess I just missed you," Cora says.

My heart squeezes at that. "I missed you, too," I say, smiling.

Maybe it's the pandemic's fault that Cora and I stopped being friends, since that's what distanced us at first. Or maybe it would've happened anyway. Shay's had different best friends over the years.

Either way, I'm glad Cora and I are friends again now. She's been so understanding, even though what I'm dealing with is so unbelievable. The fact that she believes me and is willing to help means the world. Honestly, reconnecting with her is the only silver lining of this whole mess.

I look back at my notes from that day in October, but nothing else stands out to me.

"I wonder if anything supernatural has happened in our town before," I say. "Like, maybe my house is cursed or something."

"You know, I did hear about a family that used to live in your house," Cora says. "A girl died in your bedroom."

"What?!" I almost scream before remembering we're in a library. I whisper-scream it instead.

"I'm just kidding," Cora says.

I lightly punch her in the shoulder. "Not funny."

"We could ask Ms. Harmon if she knows anything," Cora suggests.

"Good idea."

Ms. Harmon is checking out a book for someone when we get to her desk. When she's done, she asks us if we need help.

"Has anything . . . strange . . . ever happened in our town? Or in Connecticut in general?" I ask.

"What do you mean by strange?" Ms. Harmon asks.

I'm almost embarrassed to say it because what if she doesn't believe in this stuff?

"Supernatural," Cora blurts out without hesitation.

"Oh. Actually, Connecticut has quite a few urban legends," Ms. Harmon says. "We have a book on them. Let me see if it's on the shelf."

Ms. Harmon leads us to one of the nonfiction stacks. She puts on a set of reading glasses and uses her finger to scan the titles. "Ah. Here it is," she finally says.

She pulls a book out and shows it to us.

It has a dark cover showing a creepy, old house. The title says, *Connecticut Legends and Lore*.

"Thanks," I say, and bring the book back to our table.

I start by peering at the table of contents. There's a whole section on haunted cemeteries. The thought makes me shudder.

"Are there any stories about our town?" Cora asks.

After the table of contents is a map of Connecticut. There's a dot on each of the locations mentioned in the book. But none of those dots are on our town.

"Doesn't look like it," I say.

"Did you go to any other towns that day?" Cora asks.

"No. Mom and I ran all our errands around here."

The bell rings, signaling the end of lunch.

"I'm going to check this book out so I can read it after school," I tell Cora. "Do you want to meet up? At my house?"

"Yes, and yes," Cora says with a grin.


Cora's mom says she can come over after she finishes her homework, and Mom says she can join us for dinner. While I wait for Cora to come over, I finish my own math worksheets.

Her dad drops her off at the same time as the pizza is delivered, so we each eat several slices before heading upstairs to my room.

The copy of *Connecticut Legends and Lore* is on my bed.

"I have an idea that'll make this more fun," Cora says.

"We can turn off all the lights and read it using flashlights."

"I'm already freaked out by the time jump," I say. "You want to make it worse?"

"C'mon, it'll be fun. Remember that time we read that R. L. Stine book during one of our sleepovers?"

"*Goosebumps!*" I remember. "*The Haunted Mask*, I think. It was about a girl who bought a mask at a Halloween store to scare her bullies but then she became the monster."

"Right. And we'd read it in the basement!" Cora squeals, grabbing the library book and hugging it. "We have to go read this book in the basement."

"No way!" I say.

"C'mon! If you could do it when you were half your age, you can do it now."

Cora stares at me with puppy-dog eyes, still hugging the book.

"Fine," I say, cracking a smile. "But if any ghosts show up, I'm hiding behind you!"

"Deal."

When we get to the basement, Theo's down there, about to turn on his PlayStation.

"Wait—we need to do something in here," I tell him. "Can you play video games later?"

"Why?" Theo asks.

"It's something for school," I lie. "Science class. It has to be really dark for us to do the experiment. It'll take thirty minutes, tops."

Theo looks kind of annoyed, but he says, "Fine," and heads back upstairs.

I grab the remote and turn on the LED lights that are still strung around the room. "What color should I make them?"

"Red, of course," Cora says. "For blood."

"What is wrong with you!" I say.

She laughs. "Fine. How about purple?"

I switch the LED color and turn off the rest of the lights. The cool purple glow feels a lot less scary than if we'd gone with red.

Cora and I sit on the couch with the book on our laps. We use our phones' flashlights to see the pages.

"How about we each read one chapter, and then we can skim the rest?" Cora says.

"Okay. I'll go first."

The first chapter is about a lighthouse whose keeper drowned after his boat capsized in 1916, and he's now seen as an apparition who's been said to have saved people who've almost drowned.

"At least he seems like a nice ghost," I say when I'm done.

Cora reads the chapter about a sanatorium, a hospital where they treated kids with tuberculosis in the early 1900s. Paranormal researchers believe the souls of former patients are still there. Apparently if you stand outside the building at night—and even better, during a full moon—you can hear the moans and cries, and running footsteps of the former patients.

We skim through the rest of the chapters. A lot of them share stories about hauntings and ghosts. I don't think a ghost made me travel through time. But there are also stories about a supposed vampire, and a lake sea monster sighting.

"This stuff is interesting—and creepy," I say. "But I don't think we're on the right track. Nothing written here mentions time travel or the beach parking lot where the carnival took place."

The closest story from the book is about an amusement park that was in a different Connecticut town during the 1960s. When the park first opened, it was really popular. But within its first week, many of the rides malfunctioned, killing not one but three children. Turns out the rides hadn't been properly inspected. Then it was later revealed that the park was built on a former grave site. Once it eventually closed, people snuck onto the grounds to see the abandoned rides and they spotted ghosts of the dead who'd been buried there. The town decided the grounds must be haunted.

A temporary carnival isn't the same as a permanent amusement park. And this didn't even happen in our area.

"Just because it's not in the book doesn't mean weird things haven't happened at that parking lot," Cora says. "It just means nobody's documented it yet."

"I guess that's possible." I try looking up the area on my phone to see if anyone has written articles or blog posts about it, but I don't find anything supernatural.

I lean back and rest my head on the back of the couch. Cora does the same.

"We'll figure it out," Cora says.

"I hope so."


That night when I can't fall asleep, I try to think of other clues from right before the time jump. What was out of the ordinary that day?

The locket was unexpected, but I now know it came from Cora. Then I remember something else, though the memory feels hazy. Before I went to bed that night, I checked the time on the locket. It was about to turn midnight.

It felt like everything went black after that so maybe

midnight is when the time jump happened.

What else . . .

I close my eyes and try to remember every other detail.

Wasn't there a full moon that night? At the carnival, I kept looking up at the moon since it was so bright and pretty.

Connecticut Legends and Lore mentions the full moon a few times—in the sanatorium story and a couple others.

I get out of bed and go to my phone in the kitchen to look up when last October's full moon occurred. And I'm right. It was that same night.

Maybe the full moon and midnight have something to do with the time jump. Full moons are highest in the sky at midnight. I learned that when we studied the moon phases in science class last year.

And who knows—maybe the beach parking lot, where the carnival took place, was built over a grave site, or on top of a radioactive substance, or something else related to time travel. Daphne did say magic is just another kind of energy. There could be magical energy under the pavement.

What if going back to the parking lot at midnight during a full moon could give me answers?

On my phone, I look up when the next full moon will

happen. It says Thursday, April 25—only three nights away.

I text Cora and try to explain my thought process. When I write it out, it sounds far-fetched. But I still want to see if I'm onto something.

Since her parents aren't as strict about her phone, Cora might be able to text me back right away. I ask if she'll go to the carnival grounds with me on Thursday night. We'll have to figure out how to sneak out and get there, but we have time to nail down those details. Right now, I need to know if Cora is in because I can't imagine going on this wild-goose chase without her. I need her support just as much as I need answers.

I nervously pace the kitchen floor while I wait for a response. Maybe her phone isn't near her after all.

But then my phone quietly vibrates in my hand, and I see her reply.

**Count me in!**

I exhale with relief.

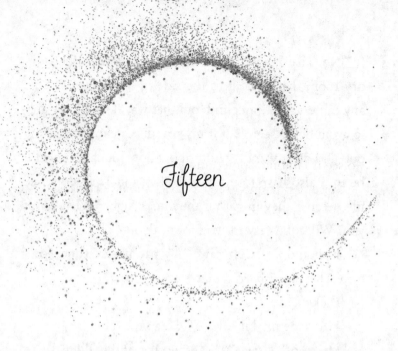

# Fifteen

Cora and I meet in the cafeteria the next day to plan.

"I want to get to the parking lot as close to midnight as possible," I say while I unwrap my sandwich. "So, we both need to sneak out. My problem is my parents have cameras around the outside of our house. There's a doorbell camera, and a camera showing the area right outside our back door. There's also a camera attached to a motion sensor light on the right side of the house. My parents get alerts on their phones whenever there's activity. They'll know if I leave the house using the front or back door."

"Do the windows have cameras, too?" Cora asks.

"No. Thank goodness. There's a window in the laundry room that lets out to the side of the house without any cameras. If I can climb out that way, I should be able to avoid being seen. But if my parents catch me sneaking out . . . I don't want to think about how much trouble I'll be in. I also have to make sure Shay and Theo don't see me because they might rat me out." I sigh. "What about you? Will it be easy for you to sneak out?"

"It should be," Cora says. "My parents are super low-tech. They don't have cameras or anything."

"Lucky."

"I can ride my bike there," Cora says.

"Me, too," I say. "That's another thing I'll have to set up ahead of time. We usually leave our bikes in the garage, but my parents will get an alert if I open that door late at night. I'll have to hide my bike in the bushes or something after school."

The good news is the beach—and the parking lot where the carnival took place—is maybe a mile from my house. So, once I get on my bike and start riding, it won't take me that long to get there.

"What will we do once we're there?" Cora asks.

"I'm not totally sure," I admit. "Before this time jump happened to me, I never believed in supernatural stuff. But now, especially after reading that library book, it must be real. I'm pretty sure the time jump happened at midnight, and that's the moment the full moon was at its highest. It must mean something. There's a reason full moons are a big deal in the fantasy books I read. There's something magical about them."

"But weren't you in your basement right before midnight?" Cora asks. "Not the parking lot?"

"Yeah," I say. "But I don't think there's anything magical about my basement. I've lived in my house my whole life, through lots of full moons, and nothing like this has ever happened before."

Cora nods.

Do I really think showing up in an empty parking lot in the middle of the night is going to fix everything? I'm not sure, but it's the only idea I have right now, and I have to do something other than read books and articles. Even if I walk away with one more clue to get me closer to the truth, it'll be worth it.

"Be honest. Do you think this will be a waste of time?" I ask Cora.

She shrugs. "I don't know. But it's worth a try and sneaking out for a nighttime adventure sounds fun." She gives a mischievous smile.

I think of all the adventure novels I've read, with protagonists who risk everything to fight a battle or discover the truth. I've never been brave enough to be adventurous like that.

But now I have a reason, a purpose.

When I go to bed on Wednesday night, I go over the next night's plan in my head. I'm so grateful that Cora has been on this journey with me. She's been there for me ever since this time jump happened. I honestly don't know what I would do without her.

I think about Melinda and Ivy, too, and wonder if maybe Cora was right. Maybe I don't need them anymore now that I have her. Melinda and Ivy were there for me last summer when I really needed a friend. I'll never forget our times together. But they aren't here for me now. Melinda chose to lie about me. Ivy chose to believe her.

And I'm still standing.

Plus, I even have Amelia back in my life now. I ended up video chatting with her again on Saturday night, hours after I got home from downtown. We decided to start our book club again and picked a fantasy graphic novel to read first. I also told her about my photography club project and how fun it's been to capture my favorite places and things on camera. Amelia told me that she signed up for a local drawing class for kids, and she wants to create her own graphic novel one day.

It still stinks that Amelia lives far away, but talking to her was so natural, like we never stopped. I guess I have to give Dream Elise credit for reconnecting us.

I still want my lost time back, since I hate that there's this other version of myself that lived my life and caused so many big changes. I want to feel in control and know that I was the one who caused my own past.

I get started on my plan as soon as I'm home from school on Thursday. First, I take my bike and helmet out of the garage and go for a short ride around the neighborhood, so it doesn't seem suspicious. When I return home, instead of parking my bike in the garage with the others, I wheel it to the left side of the house and place it between some bushes. Hopefully my parents and siblings don't come over here or pay too close attention to the bike rack in the garage.

Later, when I'm in bed and my parents come in to say good night, I'm wearing my regular pajamas. But as soon as they leave my room, I change into a black long-sleeved shirt and black leggings. Then I lie down with the lights off and wait. I need to wait for my parents to go to bed, which they usually do around 11:00 o'clock.

I listen for their bedroom door down the hall to close. When I finally hear it a little after 11:00, I crack open my door to make sure the coast is clear.

I grab the flashlight I hid under my bed, and my backpack—which I emptied and filled with a water bottle and some trail mix in case Cora and I get hungry.

At the last second, I cram a few stuffed animals and my pillows under the blanket on my bed. If my parents open my door to check on me, they'll think I'm under the blankets, sleeping. But they never check on me in bed anymore, so this is just an extra precaution. Everything must go perfectly tonight.

I open my bedroom door and slowly close it behind me, so it doesn't make any noise. I tiptoe halfway across the hall to the top of our staircase, and then walk down, careful to avoid the step that always creaks. I don't breathe until I'm finally downstairs.

But then I hear a noise—a door opening on the second floor. I shuffle around the corner from the stairs, freeze, and wait.

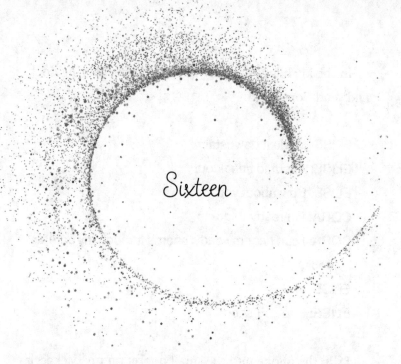

# Sixteen

I listen carefully to the footsteps above me. They walk halfway down the hall and then stop. Then it sounds like they go into the hall bathroom and close the door, which means it must be Shay or Theo. My parents have their own bathroom in their room. Still, I remain frozen in place.

After a few minutes, I hear a flush. Then the sound of the sink turning on, then off. Then a door creaking open again. Shay or Theo leaves the bathroom and walks back to their room again, closing the door.

I exhale and realize just how fast my heart was beating.

In the kitchen, I grab my phone off the charging dock and send Cora a text.

ELISE: Made it downstairs
ELISE: About to sneak out
ELISE: How about you
CORA: I'm ready to go
CORA: I can hear my dad's snores through my parents' door
ELISE: 💀
ELISE: See you soon

I slip the phone into the small pocket on my backpack and tiptoe to the laundry room. I close the door behind me and hope it'll muffle the sound of me opening the window.

Thankfully, the window opens quietly. But then I realize that I missed something major. This window has a screen on it. Of course it does! Why didn't I think to check it before? If I'd realized earlier, I could've tried to take it off after school.

I have to get it off now, somehow. And quietly. I don't know how to do that, so I grab my phone and search for "how to remove a window screen." I turn the volume all the way down and watch a video with the captions on.

After watching a couple more video clips, I learn more about window screens than I ever expected. But the good news is our window has lift tabs, which you can usually push up to pull the screen out.

Seems easy enough. I put my phone away and try what the video said.

It takes a little finagling, but it works! The bottom of the screen pops out, so I carefully pull the rest of it down and place it under the window. If tonight goes well, I won't even need to figure out how to put it back because I'll be in last October again. I crawl out the window, landing behind the bushes.

I'm outside! The hardest part is done. I lean over, put my hands on my knees, and take a few breaths. Then I grab my phone and tell Cora I'm on my way. I check the time and it's 11:23 p.m.

I wheel my bike out and walk it to the curb, careful to stay out of our front door camera's range. Then I hop on and head toward the beach.

The ride takes only about ten minutes. Along the way, the streets are empty and quiet, and the full moon shines extra bright.

When I get there, I find Cora right away. Her bike is leaned up against the fence surrounding the parking lot. She's sitting next to it with her flashlight turned on.

She stands when she sees me. "You made it."

I nod. "Barely." I give her a quick summary of what it took for me to sneak out.

"Wow," she says. "I just opened the back door and left. I don't know if I should be happy or concerned that my parents aren't more worried about security."

I shrug. "Be happy for now because we're here."

Cora looks around. "What now?"

I glance across the parking lot. Without the big carnival lights, plus all the lights from the rides, concession stands, and arcade games, it looks like one big, dark space. Even though the bright moon lightens up the parking lot a bit, I'm happy to stay close to the streetlights along the road. I get my flashlight out of my bag and turn it on, too.

"I think we should wait until midnight and see what happens." I show her my phone. "It's only eighteen minutes from now. I'll set a timer."

"Okay."

Cora and I sit back down against the fence, facing the parking lot.

I think of the stories Cora and I read in the library book—the haunted lighthouse that's across the water from here. All the spooky graveyards. What if this parking lot was built on an old grave site, and there are ghosts around here that we just can't see?

I shiver and cross my arms in front of me.

"You know," Cora says. "Even if this doesn't work, everything will be okay. Right?"

"I guess," I say, even though I'm not so sure. How will I go through the rest of my life knowing this time jump happened, but not how—or if it will happen again?

"Want to play a game while we wait?" Cora asks.

"Like what?"

She pauses to think. "Two truths and a lie?"

"Okay. You can go first."

"All right." She points the flashlight up so her face is illuminated. "One: I've never broken a bone. Two: I'm still scared of the dark sometimes. And three: My favorite memory of us is when we were seven. The town was playing a movie at the beach, and we went with our families, and we watched the sunset across this same exact parking lot. We ate way too much pizza and Popsicles, and got way too sandy, but we shared a big towel as a blanket during the movie and ended up falling asleep before it was over. The whole night was just . . . magical."

"I remember that! Is that really your favorite memory of us?" I ask.

"That's for you to guess," Cora says with a playful grin.

"The lie is . . . you're not actually scared of the dark?"

It seems like she wouldn't have agreed to come here if she was.

"Ding ding ding," Cora says.

"I loved those beach movie nights." Our town always picks animated movies for those events, so kids my age don't really go anymore.

"Your turn," Cora says.

"Okay." I think for a second. "One: I hate sushi. Two: I love ice cream. And three . . . I believe in magic."

"The first one," Cora says right away. "Everyone loves ice cream, and even if you didn't believe in it before, the fact that we're here tonight proves you believe in magic now."

I smile. "I made it too easy."

I glance down at my phone to check the time. "Oh my gosh. Only two minutes left until midnight." I stand up, not sure what I should do, but feeling like I shouldn't sit down for this. I don't know what I expect to happen once midnight hits. Will I wake up suddenly back in October? Or will something happen with the moon? All I know is spirits better not start floating out of the pavement.

I close my eyes tight and make a wish that this will work. That magic really does exist, and I can get my time back. My heart races.

"Twenty seconds," Cora says.

I open my eyes again and grab Cora's hand. I squeeze it as the timer counts down.

Five . . . four . . . three . . . two . . . one . . .

My phone alarm sounds. I let go of Cora's hand and shut it off. Then I look up at the moon. Does it look brighter? I can't tell.

Cora and I stand there in silence and wait for something to happen. We wait thirty seconds. A full minute. But nothing around us changes. It's still quiet, except for the distant sounds of insects.

I pace around as worry grows in the pit of my stomach. "Everything looks and feels the same. Maybe the full moon has nothing to do with this. Or this parking lot."

"Maybe we need to wait a little longer," Cora says.

"Or maybe coming here was a big mistake, because I'll never be able to fix this," I say, my voice getting more frantic. "Or know how it happened in the first place."

"Calm down—"

I cut her off. "I can't calm down. You don't understand how it feels to have this huge chunk of your life taken away from you, with no explanation. To have your friends suddenly hate you." I'm about to cry. I let out a loud exhale and continue pacing and wringing my hands.

"But I—" Cora starts to say.

"We should go home," I interrupt. "Maybe this does

have something to do with my basement, since that's the last place I was. I can try sleeping down there again tonight."

"Elise."

"Or maybe that won't work either because what if the magic has to do with me, Ivy, and Melinda together? But they won't agree to sleep over at my house again. They can't even look at me—"

"Elise!"

I stop pacing and look at Cora. "What?"

"I have to tell you something." Her face looks pained as she steps closer to me. "I've been . . . I've been keeping a secret. A . . . a big one."

"What kind of secret?" I ask, feeling wary.

"Promise you won't hate me?" Cora asks, suddenly looking nervous.

"Okay . . . what is it?"

"I . . ." She pauses, takes a breath, and starts again. "I know why the time jump happened."

"How?" I ask, confused. But also hopeful.

"I know," Cora says, "because I caused it. I made it happen."

My eyes widen as her words sink in, and it feels like my head might explode.

"You. *What?*"

# Part Two

## Cora

# Seventeen

I wasn't going to admit it. I didn't think I'd ever tell Elise. I couldn't. But after tonight, I can't lie to her anymore. Not when I can see how much she's hurting. She deserves to know the truth.

I'm not a friendship expert, but I know this: best friends are not supposed to keep secrets.

"You're joking, right?" Elise looks like she might laugh, or cry, or do both at the same time. "Please tell me this is a joke."

"It's not a joke." I stare right into her eyes, so she'll believe me. "I can explain everything."

*Inhale. Exhale.*

I start the story.

That night in October, I went to the fall carnival by myself. At first, I wasn't going to go at all, but after school, Mom asked me about it. She offered to drive me if I wanted to hang out there with friends from school.

What she didn't know was I didn't have any friends to hang out with. She thought I was friendly with kids from art class and photography club, because that's what I'd told her. But I don't actually talk to those kids. I keep to myself because the alternative—what I'm scared of—is that I'll be rejected.

I was going to tell Mom that I didn't want to go to the carnival. I would've been fine staying home, editing pictures, or saving more book nook inspiration photos online.

But something made me agree to go, for a little while. The part of me that was tired of feeling lonely. I couldn't keep staying home every weekend with Poppy and my crafts and expect anything to change. I had to put myself out there and stop worrying about what other people thought of me. I had to try. Even if it terrified me.

I decided to take pictures of everything while I walked around—the lights, the rides, the people, and the food.

Because of photography club, I was already spending a lot of my free time taking pictures. I'd only have my phone camera instead of Mr. G's DSLR camera, but my phone took pretty good shots.

I told myself that if I saw someone I knew, I'd talk to them. I'd try.

"Have so much fun!" Mom said way too enthusiastically when she dropped me off in the parking lot. "I'll meet you back here at eight."

"Okay." I took a deep breath and got out of the car.

The carnival was already crowded. My first instinct was to turn around and jump back into Mom's car. Instead, I forced myself to keep walking forward. I'd stay here for at least one hour before texting Mom to come get me.

I looked for things to photograph, and soon I got into a zone. I hyperfocused and got some good pictures. My favorite picture in that first batch was of younger kids on the chair swing ride with the sun setting in the background. From below, it looked like they were flying.

I saw some kids from school while I was taking pictures, but nobody I felt like talking to. Eventually I got thirsty, so I stopped to get a soda. But as I stood there drinking it, I kept noticing other groups of kids walking by me, talking and having fun. If my loneliness had felt like a rock in my stomach before, now it felt like a boulder that could crush me. I moved away from the crowds and got my phone out. I started scrolling through the pictures I'd taken and marking my favorites to edit later. This was a good distraction until I heard a group of girls laughing.

I looked up from my phone and spotted Ivy, Melinda, and Elise. Elise was wearing a sash that said, "Birthday Girl."

Oh yeah, I thought. Elise's birthday was a few days ago. I remembered one time when we were little, and she had a Halloween-themed birthday party. There were cute ghost decorations. We painted mini pumpkins and ate so much candy.

Elise looked up and made eye contact with me. She smiled, which made all my nervous energy disappear. I smiled back.

I could talk to Elise. Even though we hadn't hung out in forever, we did used to be close. She was my best friend once. The only best friend I'd had.

A quiet thought appeared in my brain. *What if she could be my best friend again?*

I walked over and started to say "Happy birthday" when Melinda cut me off. Then all three girls ran away. They said "eww" and laughed at me.

\* \* \*

"That's not true!" Elise says, interrupting my story. "We didn't run. My friends walked away, and I didn't want to lose track of them. I promise we weren't laughing at you. Ivy said something gross! That's why you heard us say 'eww.' It wasn't about you at all."

Could that be true? Did my brain trick me into thinking it was about me?

Elise shakes her head like a million things are running through her mind but she's not sure what to say first. "What does any of this have to do with the time jump?"

"I'm getting to it."

After the girls left, I started to text Mom. But the thought of asking her to pick me up only forty-five minutes after she brought me there made me feel worse about myself. So, I decided to walk back home instead.

On the way, it started to rain. It was only drizzling at first, so I kept walking, just faster. But it started raining harder, and then suddenly it was pouring. I was on Main Street by that point, so I walked up to the first store I saw with lights still on.

When I swung the door open, bells hanging from the top of the door crashed together.

They did it again when the door closed behind me.

* * *

"Daphne's Delights," Elise blurts out. "Is that the store you went to?"

I nod. "Yup."

"That's where you got my locket," she says, touching the necklace that's still hanging from her neck.

I nod again and touch my matching locket.

For a second, Elise's expression switches from anger to curiosity, so I keep going.

I was inside the store when I realized I'd never been there before. And now I was dripping water all over the floor. I stood there for a second debating whether I should go back outside and run the rest of the way home. But then I heard thunder.

Nope. I wanted to go home, but not enough to risk dying.

A woman standing by the counter said, "Welcome," and introduced herself as Daphne, the shop's owner. She was wearing shiny black leggings and a white sweater that looked super soft.

"The rain really picked up, huh?" she said once she saw how drenched I was. "Here." She passed me a cloth from behind the checkout counter.

I hesitated before taking it.

"It's clean, don't worry. It's for dusting but you can use it to dry off."

"Thanks." I wiped my hands and face, and then used it to squeeze water out of my twists.

While I did that, I looked around the shop. With the sounds of thunder and rain outside, and the moody lighting and soft music playing inside, it felt cozy. Like I was inside a meditation app or something. It made me want to take my phone out and snap some pictures.

When I was as dry as I could get, Daphne took the cloth back from me and said, "Feel free to look around while you wait out the rain. Let me know if I can help you with anything."

"Thanks," I repeated. "I'm just going to call my mom."

Mom didn't answer her cell when I called, so I sent her a text. Knowing her, she probably fell asleep on the couch and forgot to take her phone off vibrate. She also probably set an alarm to wake her up in time to pick me up at eight. That was in only a half hour so at least I wouldn't have to wait long.

I started checking out the shop. First, I went up to an incense display and smelled a few of the packages. The sandalwood one smelled nice but it made the inside of my nose itch.

"Is it okay if I take some pictures?" I asked Daphne,

who was now sitting on a stool behind the counter. "They're just for me."

"Of course," Daphne said with a smile.

I walked around the room with my phone, snapping pictures of different shelves and corners of the shop. Even though the store wasn't all that bright, I didn't use my phone's flash. Mr. G says to never use a flash indoors. I went up to the crystals display and took some macro shots—close-ups—of different ones so I could really capture the stones' details. I even took pictures of the constellation ceiling.

This place was so cool. Now I was glad the rain had forced me inside.

After a while, I put my phone away so I could get a better look at everything. I noticed a bunch of mesh pouches on one shelf, so I went over to see what they were. They each had cards hanging from a tag and were filled with various trinkets. The pouches were all different colors, and the sign above them said "Spell Kits." The red pouch was a love spell, the white pouch was a protection spell, and the green pouch was a manifestation spell. I picked up the green one and saw that it was for turning your dreams and aspirations into reality.

I wondered if there was a spell for getting over anxiety.

Or, even better, finding a best friend.

"Have you done spells before?" Daphne's voice came from behind me, making me jump in surprise.

I turned around. "No."

"If you're interested, I can help you find the right one."

"That's okay," I said.

Daphne stared at me for a second. "Sweetheart, are you sure you're all right? Is your mom coming to get you?"

"I texted her," I said. "She should be here soon."

Daphne nodded. "We close at eight but of course you can stay until your mom gets here. Is there anything I can help with before then?"

"Not unless you can get me out of middle school." I half laughed. "Do you have a spell for that?"

Daphne gave a knowing look. "I remember how awful middle school was. I was bullied so much. That's partly why I got into magic when I grew up, to feel more in control of my destiny. You're, what, in the seventh grade?"

I nodded.

"Well, I don't carry a spell about middle school specifically, but I have a bunch of different kits," Daphne said. "If there was one thing that could help you get through the seventh grade, what would it be?"

I knew my answer right away but hesitated to say it out loud. "It's embarrassing."

"I'm sure it's not," Daphne said.

"It is." My throat dried up, but I said it anyway. "I don't have a best friend. Not anymore. I wish I could have one again."

"A best friend?" Daphne's eyes lit up. "You're in luck. I have just the thing."

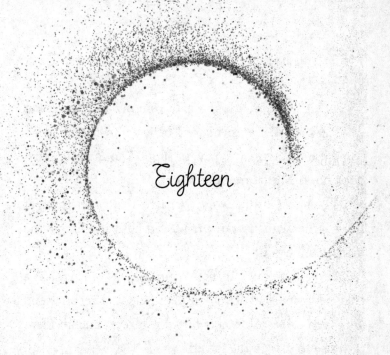

# Eighteen

Daphne scanned the shelf of spell kits and grabbed a pouch that was a pale yellow-green, like the color of sunlight filtering in through tree branches from below. She held it out to me.

I took it and read the card hanging from the outside. It said it was a friendship spell.

"Is this for real?" I asked.

Daphne nodded. "The instructions are inside. If you follow them exactly, I think you'll be pleased with the results. Your timing is perfect, too, because it's best to do spells during a full moon, like tonight. Ideally, close to midnight. But first, make sure this is what you truly want. Spells like this can be very powerful, and difficult to reverse."

The kit was $20, which I had from my allowance. But was it worth it? I wasn't sure I believed in magic, and I could use that money to pay for supplies to make my first book nook. Miniatures aren't cheap.

But what if it did work? What if that quiet thought from earlier actually came true, and Elise and I could be best friends again?

"There's one other thing," Daphne said. "Since this is a friendship spell involving another person, I recommend you use a token. An object for you to keep, and an identical one to give to the friend."

"What kind of object?" I asked.

"Anything you want. It doesn't have to be big or expensive. Just something the both of you can have, to help bring you together in friendship. The instructions in the kit say that part is optional, but I've found the spell is much more successful this way."

"Have you done this spell before?" I asked.

"I have."

"And it worked?"

Daphne nodded. "It did. But like I said, you must be careful. Choose the friend wisely."

Just then, my phone vibrated in my hoodie pocket.

It was my mom texting me back. I was right—she had fallen asleep but just saw my message.

"My mom's on her way," I told Daphne.

"Great." She smiled. "So, what do you think? Are you interested in the spell kit?"

Daphne said to choose the friend wisely, but there was really only one choice for me. I thought about how close Elise and I used to be. How much happier I was before the pandemic started and Elise moved on from me. How happy she seemed back then, too. Everything in my life would be so much better if we were still besties.

There was no way this $20 spell would do anything, but I had to admit: I was curious.

"I'll take it."

Daphne smiled again. "I'll wrap it up for you." She carried the spell kit to the register. "How about a token. Do you have something in mind?"

"Umm . . ." I couldn't think of anything off the top of my head.

But then as I was walking to the counter to pay for the spell kit, I noticed a jewelry display. One of the pieces was an oval locket necklace with a swirl design on the front. The tiny clock inside matched the time on my phone, so I knew it worked. It was beautiful. I thought of the bracelets that Elise and I made at the garage sale that one summer. We also made matching bracelets for each other, and I wore mine until it fell apart. What if Elise and I had matching lockets this time?

"Could a necklace work?" I asked Daphne, holding one of the lockets up to her.

"That's perfect. And you know what, I'm holding a sale right now. Buy one, get one free." She winked at me.

"Let me get this straight," Elise says, ripping me out of my story again. "You wanted to be friends with me again, but instead of talking to me and asking to hang out, you bought a spell kit to force me into it?"

"It's not like that!" I say, even though it does sound bad when Elise says it that way. "I didn't think the spell would work. And I didn't know that it would cause a time jump. Magic spells aren't supposed to be real!"

"I can't believe you," Elise says. "You've messed up my whole life, you know that?" She grabs on to her locket and then reaches behind her neck to unclasp it. "Next time you want to experiment with magic, do me a favor and leave me out of it." She throws the locket at me, and it hits me in my stomach before falling to the ground.

Elise picks up her bike and hops on.

"Wait!" I shout as she starts riding away. "There's more to it!"

I still haven't told her the most important part.

But it's too late. Elise is already gone.

This was a bad idea. All of it. I should never have done the spell, and I should never have told Elise. I should've kept pretending to be oblivious while I figured out a way to reverse the magic. She didn't need to know that I caused all of this to happen.

But how could I call her my best friend while also keeping this huge secret from her?

I did the spell because I wanted our friendship back, and at first, it worked! Even if it was because of the spell, it felt like we picked up right where we left off. But now everything's ruined.

Maybe Daphne can help me sort all of this out. But that'll have to wait until after school tomorrow. Or today since it's after midnight now.

I text Elise.

Please let me explain
Can we talk during lunch

A minute later, she hasn't responded. I stare at the screen hoping for three dots to appear, until the sound of a distant siren makes me jump. I shouldn't be out here by myself. I need to get out of this dark, empty parking lot.

I go to pick up my bike and spot Elise's locket lying on the pavement. I pick it up, wipe it off, and put it in my pocket. She probably won't want to wear it ever again, but I can't stand the thought of it being stepped on and crushed. Or taken and worn by someone else.

When I get home, I lean my bike against the house next to the back door and go inside. Poppy comes over right away and rubs herself against my leg. She always sleeps in my bed at night, so she must've been waiting for me. I reach down to scratch behind her ears, and she immediately purrs.

The house is quiet. Mom works nights as a baby nurse, which means a few times a week, she goes to other people's houses to help take care of their newborn babies while the parents get some rest. She's gone tonight, and Dad must still be asleep.

In my room, I change into pj's, get into bed, and wrap myself in my comforter like a burrito.

As I'm falling asleep, I think back to that October night—all the things that happened after Mom finally picked me up from Daphne's Delights. I came home, changed into dry, cozy clothes, and then opened the spell kit to see what was inside.

There was a booklet with instructions, a small candle with a holder, and a stone the same pale yellow-green color as the pouch the kit came in. I opened the booklet and on the first page, under the list of contents, it said the crystal was a peridot, which apparently represents friendship.

I read the instructions for the spell and remembered that Daphne said it was best to perform it around midnight. In the meantime, I could give the token to the person I wanted to become my friend. Daphne had included a small gift box and bag, so I put one of the lockets inside.

My parents couldn't drive me since they know Elise's parents and would definitely ask questions. So, I snuck out and rode my bike to her house. I didn't want anyone at her house to see me deliver the gift, so I quickly dropped the bag on her front porch doormat while hiding my face from the doorbell camera.

By 11:00 that night, my parents were in their bedroom, and at 11:30, I went downstairs to start setting up the spell. It honestly felt a little silly, but I'd already bought the stuff and had nothing better to do. Plus, it was a full-moon night. The moon looked super bright.

I wasn't about to burn the house down, so I brought everything outside to the backyard. I put a towel down on the damp grass next to the stepping stones that led to the front of the house and sat on it. I put the candle in the center of one stone and lit it with a lighter stick I found in the junk drawer. While the flame flickered, I grabbed a piece of paper and wrote Elise Jackson on the top. Beneath that, I wrote down my biggest wish—for us to become best friends again.

I held the paper over the flame and let it catch fire. It burned while I held it for a few seconds. Then I let it drop onto the stone. It kept burning until the paper was a small pile of embers. Meanwhile, the candle continued flickering in its holder.

The next step, according to the instructions, was to hold on to the peridot stone, as well as my token—the locket—and repeat the incantation seven times out loud. I squeezed my locket in my right hand. I made sure the incantation was open in front of me so I could read off the words. Then I squeezed the peridot stone in my left hand.

"Moonlight shining bright," I started, saying each word carefully and quietly. "Unite us with this light. As we begin anew, make this friendship true."

I took a breath and started again.

"Moonlight shining bright, unite us with this light. As we begin anew, make this friendship true."

By the third time, I'd memorized the incantation. I repeated it the next few times with my eyes closed, still holding the locket and peridot stone. I imagined me and Elise as best friends, like we never stopped.

Even though part of me felt like this was a ridiculous waste of time, there was another part that wished it would work.

I said the incantation one last time and sat there watching the candle flicker for a while. Then I blew it out.

Before I went to bed, I put my locket on. By then I was so tired that I quickly fell into a deep sleep.

The next morning, I woke up feeling confused. My school alarm, which was only scheduled to go off on weekday mornings, had gone off.

But it was Sunday. Wasn't it?

It wasn't. It was a Monday, six months later.

Before Elise stormed off, I didn't get to tell her that she wasn't the only one who jumped ahead in time.

I did, too.

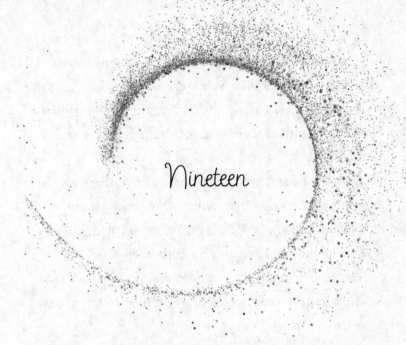

# Nineteen

*I check my phone as* soon as I wake up the next morning to see if Elise texted me back. But there are no new messages.

My heart sinks.

She still might meet me in the cafeteria during lunch. Even though I'm exhausted from going to sleep after midnight, I jump out of bed and quickly get dressed for school. I wear my locket and put Elise's in my backpack pocket in case she wants it back after we talk.

When I walk into the kitchen, Mom is packing my lunch while still wearing her scrubs from last night's baby nursing shift. These scrubs are light blue with baby ducks all over them. Mom always wears cute scrubs to work.

"Here you go, sweetie." She yawns and hands me the brown paper bag. She usually goes to bed for a few hours after I leave for school, so she's awake again by the time I get home.

"Thanks," I say, yawning back at her.

"Why are *you* yawning?" Mom asks. "Did you not sleep well?"

"Something like that," I say.

"At least it's Friday. You can sleep in tomorrow."

"Yeah." Then I ask, "Can I go downtown after school? I want to go back to that store where I got my locket."

"Sure," Mom says.

We both yawn again and laugh.


On the walk to school, I think back to a few weeks ago—the morning after the time jump.

When my alarm rang that morning, I woke up super groggy and confused. I thought something was wrong with my clock. I went into the hallway and heard the morning news playing from the TV in my parents' bedroom. A voice said that it was going to be a beautiful spring day, with partly cloudy skies and a high of 52 degrees.

*Spring day?*

I walked into their room to see what date was on the screen. In the bottom right corner, next to the time, it said April 8.

I sat on the edge of my parents' bed. Last night it was October and this morning it was April. I thought of the spell, the last thing I did before I went to sleep. It had to have something to do with this.

"Morning, baby," Dad said once he noticed me. He was picking out a button-down shirt from his closet.

"Morning," I said. "What day was it yesterday?"

I watched him glance at the TV screen. "April seventh. Sunday." He looked at me. "Why?"

"No reason." I went back to my room to get ready for school.

While I was getting dressed, I started to worry. What if the spell didn't work? What if I did it wrong? It was supposed to be a friendship spell, not a time-travel spell.

I went to my trash can, where I'd thrown out the leftover items from the spell kit. But they weren't there. I knew this is where I left them, so they should've been at the top of the pile.

But that was back in October. It was apparently April now.

The spell kit stuff was long gone.

I needed to talk to Daphne. She would know what was

happening. I could go straight to her shop after school.

Before then, there was only one way to know for sure if the spell worked.

I needed to find Elise.

I vibrated with nerves and excitement as I walked to school. What would Elise do when she saw me? Would it be obvious that we were best friends again?

I couldn't find her before the first bell rang, and I didn't see her in the hall between any of my classes. At one point I spotted Melinda and Ivy talking to each other, but they were by themselves.

I felt disoriented during my first classes as I realized I'd missed a ton of lessons. But if the spell actually worked, I could deal with that.

As soon as the bell rang for the seventh-grade lunch period, I hurried to the cafeteria. Instead of grabbing a seat at a table by the window, like I normally did, I waited by the entrance, so I'd see Elise as soon as she walked in.

And then I saw her. She stepped into the cafeteria like she was on a mission. Like she was looking for someone.

For me?

"Hi, Elise," I said, giving her my friendliest smile.

She looked surprised to see me. "Oh, uh. Hey . . ." She flashed a smile but kept peering around the cafeteria.

Before I could say anything else, or ask if she wanted

to sit with me, she said, "I'm so sorry. I've gotta go." Then she walked away—right to where Melinda and Ivy were sitting.

I stood there, stunned. Embarrassed. And furious.

Daphne scammed me! The spell hadn't made Elise into my best friend. *And* it made me travel through time. This was not what I asked for!

I glanced at Elise as I walked to my usual seat, and that's when I noticed something was happening with Melinda and Ivy at their table. I wasn't close enough to hear what they were saying, but Melinda seemed angry and Ivy looked uncomfortable. Then they got up and stormed off without Elise.

*Hmm.* Maybe the spell was working after all. But then guilt rose in my chest as I saw how confused and upset Elise looked while watching her friends walk away from her. If the spell caused this, that was terrible. The last thing I wanted was to *hurt* Elise.

That afternoon I went to the photography club meeting and found out that Elise was supposed to be there, too. Mr. G asked me about her. She must've joined the club during the months I missed. Elise never showed up, maybe because she was still upset about what happened during lunch.

I hated feeling like I didn't know everything that was

going on in photography club. Apparently, we'd started our photo essays, and I'd taken pictures at Dad's theater. I didn't recognize any of them. This was so weird. I tried to act normal while Mr. G taught about depth of field.

After photography club, I asked Mom if I could stop by Daphne's Delights. She agreed and waited in the car for me. I walked into the shop, and Daphne was wrapping up some crystals for a customer, an older woman. There was a purple one with jagged edges, a smooth turquoise one, and a shiny egg-shaped one.

She smiled when she saw me. "I'll be with you in a second."

While I waited, I looked around the shop to see if anything had changed since I was last here. It looked exactly the same, only this time, it wasn't storming outside. The daytime light changed the vibe somewhat, but it still felt magical. I was tempted to take out my phone again to snap some more pictures.

"Cora," Daphne said when the other customer had finally left. "I wondered when I'd see you again. I waited to hear from you back in October, but when you didn't come, I thought either you didn't perform the spell. Or . . ."

"Or I jumped to a different month altogether?" I asked.

Daphne nodded.

"When I went to bed last night, it was October," I said. "And now it's April. What's going on?" I was about to ask for my money back, but it was more than that. I wanted my time back.

"I think it's a good sign that the spell is working," Daphne said.

"Are you serious? Then why didn't Elise . . . the girl I chose for the spell . . . act like it today at school? She barely said hi to me."

"Magic can only do so much," Daphne explained. "It can cause tweaks and nudges in our lives, but it cannot replace free will."

"*What?*" I asked.

"Imagine you're hiking in the woods, and several of the paths you can take are hidden by shrubs," Daphne said. "What magic can do is help identify a path for you, by moving the shrubs out of the way and adding more sunlight. It makes the path more desirable and shows you the way, but you still have to decide on your own to walk that path."

"So . . . in this analogy, I'm the path that Elise has to choose?" I asked, annoyed that Daphne hadn't explained this when I bought the spell.

"Precisely. The spell must've seen a way for your friendship to develop, months in the future. So, it jumped you ahead in time, setting a path where it's ideal for you and Elise to come together as friends."

"Do you think Elise jumped ahead in time, too?" I asked.

"I wish I could tell you for sure," Daphne said.

"Well, why did the spell bring me to the future instead of the past?" I asked. "If it brought me back to the start of the pandemic when me and Elise were still friends, maybe I could've changed what happened next."

"You wouldn't have been able to change Elise's actions back then," Daphne explained. "But the future is still unwritten, so the magic brought you here—and now."

I mentioned how Elise's other friends seemed to reject her in the cafeteria earlier. "Was that because of the spell? Did I cause that?"

Daphne shook her head. "Remember what I said about free will. Magic can't make anyone do anything."

I nodded, feeling somewhat better. If what happened with Elise's friends would've happened even without my friendship spell, then I guess I didn't need to reverse it. But I still felt uncertain about what to do next.

It was like Daphne read my mind, because she said, "It sounds like Elise needs a friend now more than ever. What happens next is up to you."

# Twenty

The betrayal on Elise's face from the beach parking lot last night is burned into my brain like a Polaroid. I need to talk to her and make things right. When I get to school, I go straight to her locker, but I don't see her. I peek at my phone one more time before my first class. She still hasn't responded to my text.

During lunch, I go to the cafeteria and find our usual seat. I watch the minutes tick by on the clock above the door, while my stomach grumbles for my lunch. But I'm too antsy to eat.

Finally, the bell rings. Lunch is over, and Elise never

shows. She must've stayed home from school today. I can't blame her.

I scarf down some of my lunch while I walk to my next class.

It seems like my only hope at this point is to talk to Daphne again. I realize now how big of a mistake this was. Of course, a magical spell wasn't the right way to become best friends with Elise again. I never thought it would make Elise jump ahead in time, but once I realized it had, I should've tried to reverse it right away.

I thought if Elise and I got close, she'd forget about Melinda and Ivy. She said it herself—she only became friends with them last year. We were friends for much longer than that when we were younger. And once I heard how Melinda lied about Elise, it made even more sense to me for Elise to move on from them.

But that wasn't my choice to make. How could I be so selfish?

I wasn't thinking about what Elise really wanted, only what would be good for me. I missed her and didn't want to lose her a second time. But that's not a good excuse.

Before, when I was lonely, I felt sorry for myself but still liked who I was. I knew I was a good person. I can't say that now.

Hopefully Daphne can help me reverse the spell, so Elise and I can both get back to October.

When I get home from school, Mom drops me off downtown. I walk into Daphne's Delights and see the last person I expect.

Elise.

She's standing at the checkout counter next to Daphne. They both glance at me when I walk in, but neither seems surprised to see me.

"Welcome back, Cora," Daphne says, like she was expecting me to show up.

"Thanks . . ." I peer around the shop and see that we're the only ones in the store right now. *Good.* Daphne can help us reverse the spell with no other customers to distract her, and Elise and I can move on with our lives.

"You were asking," Daphne says to Elise.

"Yeah. What kind of place is this?" Elise asks, her hand on her hip. "Are you some kind of witch?"

Daphne laughs. "No. I'm not a witch. I'm a person like you. I just know how to use magic. I opened this shop to service those who want to improve their lives using more . . . unconventional methods."

"How are you allowed to sell magic spells to any random person who walks in?" Elise asks. "To kids? Is this even legal?"

"Our government doesn't have laws regarding magic," Daphne explains. "How could they? Most people don't even believe in it. But for those who do, I provide the tools they need."

"Why was I able to do the spell?" I ask. "I didn't really believe in magic before. I kind of thought the spell was a joke."

"Even though you thought it wasn't real, the magic worked because there's a part of you that believes," Daphne says. "The spell would've failed otherwise. Kids in general are more likely to be able to harness magic because your mind is still open to the possibilities of the unknown. In other words, kids your age believe in it more than adults do."

"I still think what you're doing here is super sketchy," Elise says. "But what I really want to know is if the spell Cora did can be reversed."

"It's difficult to reverse," Daphne says. "But not impossible."

"Thank. Goodness," Elise says with a huge sigh.

Even though I know that's why Elise came here, and that this is the right thing to do, it still hurts. Reversing the spell means going back to when we weren't friends anymore. To when I felt so alone.

"Cora, when did you perform the spell?" Daphne asks.

"Last October, toward the end," I say. "I think it was the twenty-second."

Daphne nods. "There was a full moon that night, correct?"

"Yes. You said the spell would work the best during a full moon, and close to midnight, so that's when I performed it. Then I woke up the next day, and it was April."

"Wait a minute," Elise says slowly. "You jumped ahead in time, too?"

I give her a look. "I tried to tell you last night before you stormed off."

Elise's eyes widen as she takes this in. "I need to sit down."

Daphne motions to the stool behind the counter, and Elise sits on it.

"You'll need to wait for the next full moon to reverse the spell," Daphne says. "And if I have my math right . . ." She pauses to think. "Yes, the next full moon will be the seventh one since the spell was placed. So that night will be your one and only chance to reverse it."

"Wait. *Why?*" Elise asks. "What does the seventh full moon have to do with anything?"

"Seven is a very powerful number in magic," Daphne explains. "Haven't you noticed it everywhere? There are seven days in the week, seven colors of the rainbow, seven notes in a major scale, seven continents. Magic follows natural patterns. With magic, the farther you get from a spell, the harder it can be to reverse. And once you've gone through seven moon cycles, it's impossible. The spell becomes permanent."

Permanent.

Elise will never forgive me if I can't reverse this spell. Knowing she hates me is so much worse than when she just didn't notice me anymore.

"I just want this to be fixed," Elise says. "I want my life back the way it was. If we have to wait until the next full moon to reverse the spell, that's another whole month, since we had a full moon last night. Is that right?"

"Correct," Daphne says. "That's the best chance you have of it working."

"But also, if the spell reversal doesn't work on that night, it won't be able to be reversed at all?" Elise asks.

"It's unlikely," Daphne says.

Elise shakes her head. "This is insane."

"What do I have to do to reverse it?" I ask Daphne. "Is there a kit for that?"

"I'll put one together for you and have it ready before the next full moon. But there's one other issue."

"What?" I ask.

"Undoing a spell is tricky. Magic doesn't like to move

backward in time. But in this case, you're lucky that it would be reversing its own steps." She glances at us and sees our confused looks. "In the 'path in the woods' analogy I gave you earlier, I explained that magic opened up one of the many paths you and Elise could walk down. For magic to go back now and undo its own work, it needs to cover the path again—including your own footsteps. It needs to set everything back to the way things were before the spell was performed."

"I definitely want to go back to the way things were before," Elise says.

"Me, too," I say, and I mean it. This has all been a mistake. Things are worse than ever. I want to go back to October—to before I ruined everything. To when I was invisible, which would be easier than being hated now.

"It's good that you want this," Daphne says. "But this means you need to be aligned in your desires. You both have to decide to walk back on this 'path' you chose, to be united and work together to reverse it. You'll need to get along. All this tension and hostility I'm feeling between you will stand in your way. If you can't unite quickly, the spell's magic will continue working to find another way to unite you."

"What does that mean?" Elise asks tentatively, like she's afraid of hearing the answer.

"Magic is finicky and impatient," Daphne says. "The spell promised a friendship. If you don't find a way to become friends again—or succeed in reversing the original spell—the magic will take over again."

"Meaning?" I ask. "Could you be more specific?"

"*Meaning*," Daphne says. "The magic could cause something else unpredictable to happen. Like move you two forward again, to another future time."

Elise's eyes go wide, and I feel like I've been dunked in ice-cold water.

*Another* time jump?

What have I done?

# Twenty-One

"That can't happen," Elise says to Daphne. "No way. You've got to help us." She's pleading at this point.

"I don't want that to happen either," I say quickly.

"I suggest you come together and get on the same page, then," Daphne says.

"How will we know when we're united?" I ask.

Daphne thinks for a second, and then her face lights up with an idea. "Do you still have your matching lockets? Can I see them?"

Elise shakes her head no, but I unclasp mine from around my neck.

"I have yours, too." I pull it out of my backpack pocket

and hand both lockets to Daphne.

Elise crosses her arms uncomfortably, but still doesn't look at me.

"Great," Daphne says. She cups both lockets between her hands and closes her eyes.

Elise and I stare at her quietly, waiting for something to happen.

Daphne's mouth starts moving, like she's saying something, but no sound comes out. With her eyes still closed, and the lockets still clasped between her hands, she mouths words for another minute or two. She looks like she's really concentrating.

I hold my breath until I can't anymore, and then I take another breath and hold that.

Finally, Daphne stops. She opens her eyes and her hands. I gasp when I notice that the lockets are glowing. But the light around them fades when Daphne holds them out to us.

"What just happened?" Elise asks as she takes hers.

"I put a spell on the lockets," Daphne says. "If you look at the clocks inside, you'll see that the big and little hands are rotating. You'll know that you're ready to reverse the spell once they stop moving."

I open my locket and sure enough, the clock hands are spinning around and around. Not too fast, but like some invisible force is adjusting the time.

"What if they don't stop rotating before the next full moon?" Elise asks.

"Then you won't be able to reverse the spell," Daphne says. "But the full moon is weeks away. You have time to unite in your desires."

I nod and glance at Elise, but she still won't look in my direction.

"We're never going to get on the same page if you can't even look at me," I tell her.

"Don't blame this on me," Elise says, making eye contact finally. It's the first time she's looked at me since she threw her locket last night.

I wish I could go back to the minute before I opened my mouth in the parking lot and told the truth.

"You're the one who started this, who did the spell in the first place," Elise says. "Then lied to me for weeks while pretending to be my friend."

"I wasn't pretending!" I say. But I know she's not entirely wrong. I did something terrible by misleading her. I wanted to be friends again so badly that I forgot how to actually be a good friend.

"And now you're still lying," Elise says. "You don't want to reverse the spell because you want to keep manipulating me."

"That is not true! I *do* want to fix this," I say. "I mean, do I look happy right now? Everything is messed up, for both of us. I know that the time jump is my fault and I'm really, really sorry, both for causing it and for not being honest about it. Please believe me." Hot tears sting my eyes, but I breathe in big gulps of air to stop them from falling. The last thing I want to do is cry in front of Elise.

Instead of accepting my apology, she says, "I don't understand. Why'd you tell me the truth, anyway? If you hadn't said anything, I probably wouldn't have figured it out."

"Because I didn't want to keep lying to you," I say. "Because I loved being your friend again, even though I didn't mean for this to happen. And real friends don't lie to each other. And I wanted it to be *real*. I wanted it to be real so badly, like it was when we were little. And you have no idea how much I wish I'd never magicked us into this." My voice cracks, and I clear my throat.

Elise shakes her head, and we're both quiet for a minute, staring at each other. All the secrets are finally out.

I realize that Daphne has been watching us argue. It suddenly feels like it's a million degrees in here, and my brain is telling me to flee.

But I need to get through to Elise first.

"I know you don't believe me, but I really am sorry," I tell her. "I made a mistake, and now I want to fix it."

"You're right," Elise says. "I don't believe you."

I let out a frustrated sigh. "You know what I think? Maybe it's you. Maybe we're not 'united' in this because you finally realized that Melinda and Ivy aren't the good friends you thought they were. They may not say mean things out loud, but I know you see how they turn their bodies away, how they share snarky looks, how they judge others. I don't think you actually want to go back to that. And maybe that scares you."

Elise looks stunned, then angry. Like she's trying to think of what to say back. When she doesn't immediately reply, I know I'm onto something. But then her eyes narrow, and she says, "I want to go back to October, but that doesn't mean I'll go back to being friends with them." She looks me right in my eyes and adds, "It just means I can go back to avoiding *you*."

My throat gets tight, and my mouth drops open.

I don't need this. I don't need her. Maybe I've been wrong about her this whole time.

Right then, the door to the shop opens, and the bells chime. Three teenage girls walk in, and they're each holding cups from the local coffee shop.

"This is the best store," one of them says. "Come smell these candles."

"Welcome," Daphne calls out to them. She begins heading over, but then turns back to me and Elise. "Girls," she says in a low voice. "If you want to reverse the spell, you need to work this out. You need to stop fighting. Come back before the next full moon, and I'll have the reversal kit ready for you."

I guess that's our cue to leave. We sheepishly nod at Daphne and walk out of the shop, Elise leading the way.

Out on the sidewalk, we stand a couple of feet away from each other. I text Mom to let her know I'm ready to be picked up. Elise is on her phone, too, so she's probably also messaging her ride. A minute later, she puts her phone away.

"We have to find a way to make the magic think we're together on this," I say.

"How do you expect us to do that?" Elise asks.

I stare at a couple across the street walking their two corgis in matching checkered bandannas.

"Daphne said if we don't act like friends, the magic could do something drastic," I say. "So, we could pretend to be friends."

"You mean trick the magic?"

I shrug. "It's worth a try. We could eat lunch together at school. Try to get along."

"Fine," Elise says, sounding exasperated. "I'll see you at school. I've gotta go."

Then she turns and walks away.

The play Dad produced has its opening night tonight. Mom doesn't have to work, so we go to see the show together after grabbing Indian food from the restaurant a few doors down from the theater. It's our tradition whenever Dad has a new play. Before the show starts, we stop by backstage to say hi to him.

Dad says the "best seats in the house" are in the center of the third row in the orchestra, so that's where Mom and I sit. I watched some of the play during the dress rehearsal last weekend, but I was too focused on taking pictures to pay attention to the story. This will be my first time seeing the whole thing, and I'm glad to have something to distract me tonight. While we're waiting for the lights to dim and the curtain to lift, we look at the program. I hold it out in front of me and snap a photo of it, with the stage in the background. I wonder if I should start using the Booster account Elise helped me create to share some of my photos.

"You know, you could've invited Elise tonight," Mom

says as I'm flipping through the program. "Dad could've gotten her a ticket."

I sink down in my seat. I don't want to tell Mom that I'm not friends with Elise anymore. Not when she was so excited once we started hanging out again after so long. How can I admit that I messed it all up, and that it was never real?

I look around us. All the seats in our row, and in the rows in front and behind us, are full.

"I think the show's sold out," I finally say.

Mom nods. "I'll tell her mom that we can get them complimentary tickets sometime. We're grabbing coffee next week."

*Great.*

This is another reason to get back to October. My parents can forget about Elise and her family again.

I try to lose myself in the play, which is entertaining, but I still feel icky, like my skin is crawling. There's the shame from messing things up with Elise, and the feeling like I'll never find another friend like her. That I'll never be good enough for someone to call me their best friend again.

By the time the play is over, I'm ready to go home and crawl into bed. Mom and I make our way out of the theater and find Dad in the lobby.

"The show was fantastic," Mom says.

"Yeah, Dad," I say, putting on a smile. "I loved it."

He hugs us both. "Thank you. I'll be ready to go for ice cream in about ten minutes."

That's our other opening-night tradition—ice cream after the show.

"Actually, can we go another night instead?" I ask.

Mom and Dad look at me, surprised. I guess I've never said no to ice cream before.

"I'm just tired," I add.

Thankfully they agree. Back home, I cuddle in bed with Poppy, the only friend I have right now. If only she could talk.

I try to do the things I usually like before bed, like looking through photos I've taken that day, editing them with an app, and searching for book nook inspiration. But nothing is loosening this pit in my stomach.

I don't think I'll feel happy again until this spell is reversed. I just have to get through the next few weeks until the full moon. And then this will be over.

## Twenty-Two

Elise and I do eat lunch together on Monday—but that's all we do. We chew and munch, and sip our drinks, but don't say a word to each other for the first half of the period. I keep waiting for Elise to say something, and I guess she's waiting on me.

"We're not going to trick the magic into thinking we're friends if we don't talk," I finally say.

"Fine," Elise says. "I'll talk. I have a question anyway."

She turns to face me for the first time since we sat down. "Why did you pick me for the spell? Is it just because you saw me the night of the carnival?"

I shake my head. "I wasn't lying when I told you I

missed you. I really did. I missed everything from when we used to be best friends."

"Oh."

"Can I ask you a question now?" I ask.

She nods.

"Why did you stop being my friend in the fourth grade?" I ask. "Did I do something wrong?"

"Why would you think you did something wrong?" Elise asks.

"Because all of a sudden, you didn't want to hang out with me anymore."

Elise shakes her head. "It wasn't like that. Once the pandemic started, we weren't allowed to get together. We were all stuck at home."

"Right, but after that," I say. "Once we went back to school in the fall . . ."

"We weren't in the same class," Elise says, a little defensively. "Then I met Amelia and started hanging out with her more. You and I just grew apart."

"You grew apart from me," I correct her. "Even once it was safe to get together again, you didn't want to hang out with me anymore. When I reached out, you were always too busy with Amelia. Other kids went through the pandemic and stayed friends. Why couldn't we?"

"So, you're punishing me because I made a new friend?"

"I'm not punishing you," I say. "I'm trying to understand what happened."

"So much happened back then," Elise says. "With the pandemic, everything was different and scary. I didn't stop being friends with you on purpose. It just happened. You need to move on."

"Like you need to move on from Melinda and Ivy?" I snap.

She scowls at me, and I scowl back.

Then she gathers her stuff and stands up.

"Just so you know, the only reason I'm still talking to you right now is because I want to reverse this stupid spell," she says. "I'll see you at photography club."

I watch her leave, and then peek at the clock in my locket. I'm not surprised that the hands are still spinning.

Elise and I are more divided than ever.

When the last bell of the day rings, I head to Mr. G's classroom. I can't wait to lose myself in Photoshop for the next hour. Plus, whatever else Mr. G teaches us today.

"Hi, Cora," Mr. G says as I flip through the folders to find mine.

"Hi," I say.

I bring my folder and a laptop to my usual desk. Elise is already here, at the desk next to mine.

"Hey," I say.

"Hey," she says, but it's the least enthusiastic "hey" ever.

While my laptop boots up, I peer at Elise through the corner of my eye. She's hunched over in her seat, resting her chin in her palm as she flips through photo prints. She seems sad. And lonely. I should know because it's exactly how I feel.

I take my prints out of my folder and start going through them. But it's hard to focus. Now that I'm here, it doesn't feel like this photo essay matters much. With everything else going on, and with the threat of another time jump hanging over Elise and me. Who cares if my theater pictures look perfect when magic might rip me away from this moment, any moment?

"Welcome back, photographers," Mr. G says from the front of the room.

Everyone stops what they're doing to pay attention.

"With only three weeks left until our showcase," Mr. G continues, "you should hopefully have all the pictures you need for your photo essays. If you're missing any, please take them this week. I want to spend our remaining time editing our photos and putting them in an order that will have the biggest impact. To help with this, I'm going to group you in pairs so you can critique each other's essays and give constructive feedback. What I mean by *constructive* is your comments must offer a *useful* suggestion to make their photo essay better. No mean comments, okay?"

I'm not surprised when Mr. G pairs Elise and me together. She doesn't object, but she also doesn't look at me.

Mr. G tells us to use the rest of the meeting to start critiquing each other's photo essays, and then set a time to meet again before next week's meeting. The room fills with voices as the other partners get to work.

"Want to look at your pictures first?" I ask Elise. Even if this feels kind of trivial, I still want Mr. G to see that I'm trying.

"Fine." She slides her stack of prints over to me.

I flip through them, recognizing the ones we took together at Sunny's Books. One of the pictures she took on her own is a shot of the mural in the bookstore's children's section. Colorful book silhouettes create a rainbow on the wall above a shorter shelf that holds a bunch of picture books with equally vibrant spines.

She also took a photo showing an overview of the shop from above.

"I love this one. How did you get that angle?" I ask.

Elise shrugs. "Beth let me kneel on the counter for a second to take it."

"That's really cool." When I'm done flipping through all the pictures, I go through them one more time while I think of some constructive criticism. "Mr. G wants our essays to tell a story, right? You have some awesome shots of the store, but I wonder if you could pick a point of view for some of the pictures. Like, are you showing the bookstore from a customer's point of view?"

Elise doesn't say anything, just shrugs.

Okay . . .

"You know what could be fun?" I ask. "If it was from Sunny's point of view. Like, a day in the life of a bookstore dog."

Still no response. Why is she even here if she's not going to try?

"You could still use some of these pictures," I continue. "Maybe start with nice shots of the store, and then focus on Sunny." I pause and wait for Elise to react. When she doesn't, I say, "It's just an idea."

Elise nods. "Thanks."

If this is her way of getting back at me, it's working.

"Should we talk about mine now?" I give Elise's photos back and then hand her my folder. I watch as she flips through my pictures. She's quiet for so long, I start to wonder if she'll say anything at all.

But then she finally says, "I didn't know you were into plays and stuff."

"Oh, I'm not really," I say. "Well, that's not true. I like the theater. My dad works at this one, so I get to hang out backstage sometimes. But it's not my passion or anything."

Elise nods again. "I don't really have any other comments."

"Seriously?" I ask.

"You're good at this," she says, matter-of-fact. "Your pictures are all good."

"Thanks . . ." I don't know what else to say. We sit in silence afterward.

Mr. G reminds us to bring our photo folders home and decide on a time to meet with our partner again before next week. Elise and I agree to meet again on Saturday afternoon. I hope we'll be able to get along better, since we only have so much time before the next full moon.

Later on, after I'm done with my homework, I lay out my photo essay pictures on my bed. I have to move Poppy out of the way when she tries to walk across them to get to my pillow, where she likes to curl up.

As I'm looking through them, I think about Elise's one

comment—that she thought I photographed Dad's theater because I'm into plays. I probably should've picked something more personal for my essay. Elise photographed the bookstore because it's her favorite place and she loves to read. Maybe I should've photographed Get Crafty, my favorite art supply store.

I open the photos folder on my phone and scroll through all the pictures I've taken since the time jump. I pause when I get to the picture Elise took of the two of us outside Sunny's Books. Looking at our two faces, smooshed together and smiling, makes a lump form in my throat.

But then I get an idea and open my phone's camera.

# Twenty-Three

*If I could live inside* a craft store, I totally would. But since I can't, the next best thing has been making my room *feel* like the inside of one.

One corner of my room is my sleeping and chill area, with my daybed covered in pillows, soft blankets, and several small stuffed animals that I crocheted. The rest of my room is for making stuff. Before I got into photography, I did a lot of crochet and hand lettering, so I have a bunch of supplies in bins on my bookshelf—crochet needles, notepads, plus stickers and washi tape. A few other bins are bursting with colorful skeins of yarn. I have jars filled with watercolor markers in every color on my desk. A magnetic bulletin board that spans the wall above my desk is filled with quotes I've hand drawn, favorite pictures I've taken, crochet patterns I plan to work on, and a big list of supplies that I want to add to my collection soon.

I haven't forgotten about my book nook frame, which sits on my bookshelf next to my craft books. I've been keeping a list of items to buy for it, like fairy lights, acrylic paint, and brushes. I need to settle on a design before I figure out what else I'll need.

Around my room are some other fun things that I've collected over time, like a mirror on the wall above my bed that looks like a bowl of ramen, and a giant plastic crayon leaning against a corner. Some people might think my room is "a lot" but my mom likes to say it's whimsical. All I know is being in here makes me happy.

Nobody gets to see my room except my parents, and my cousins whenever they visit. Elise was the first friend in a long time to come up here.

I could've used my room for my photo essay and photographed all the quirky details. But other kids would probably think it's weird. My room is my oasis, and not for anyone else to judge.

Although now I have an even better idea for a side project.

I go into my closet and take out a ring light, which I got at the beginning of the school year. I thought I'd use it to take pictures of other people for photography club. But then the time jump happened, and my . . . time jump self . . . never used it. It's still in the box it came in. I remove all the packaging and set it up so it's facing my desk area. It has a phone holder, so I stick my phone in and adjust the settings on the ring light and my phone, so the lighting looks good. Then I set up the self-timer on my phone's camera and hurry over to my desk. I lean against it and give a small smile as the phone counts down and takes the shot.

I wasn't lying when I told Elise that I'm not into selfies. I never take pictures of myself. So, I'm nervous when I look at my phone's screen to see how this one came out.

It's not bad. The lighting is fine, but I should move over a little. And I need a better facial expression. I look sort of scared. Probably because I am. Maybe I need a prop to hold on to. I look around my desk until my eyes land on a postcard-sized paper with "creativity takes courage" handwritten on it in the brush lettering technique I've been practicing. I actually first saw the phrase on a poster in Mr. G's classroom. It's perfect since I feel like I'm using all my bravery to do this right now.

I get my phone camera ready again and take a few more shots, this time holding the postcard between my thumb and fingers. By the last one, I think I've nailed it. I'm smiling more confidently, while still looking relaxed, and you can see that I'm surrounded by my craft supplies. I send the best photo to my laptop and use Photoshop to make some adjustments. Then I hit print.

I'm happy with it. Then I think of another idea. This time, I move the ring light next to my bed. I need more height. I can't put the light on my desk chair because the soft cushion won't hold it up. So, I run downstairs to the kitchen.

Dad's there, taking ingredients out of the fridge for dinner. "What are you up to?" he asks when I pick up one of our wooden dining chairs and start walking out of the room with it.

"I need this for something upstairs."

He puts down a bag of potatoes. "Let me help you."

"Okay."

Dad helps me carry the chair upstairs to my room.

"Thanks," I say once he sets it down.

"Is this for your photography project?" he asks, eyeing the ring light. "I thought you got everything you needed at the theater."

"I did. This is just a side project. For me."

Dad nods. "Well, I can't wait to see it."

I don't tell him that I probably won't share this with anyone.

When he leaves, I put the ring light on the chair and adjust the stand as high as it can go. Then I position my phone in the holder again, this time facing it down toward my bed.

I grab some yarn and spread the skeins around my daybed, forming a colorful arch. I also spread my crochet animals around. There's an octopus, turtle, owl, bunny, peacock, and multicolored chameleon. I crocheted a few foods, too, like an avocado and strawberry. I also crocheted a cupcake that I ate when my family visited Boston last summer. It was Froot Loop flavored, with cereal pieces on top. The actual cupcake was delicious, and the crocheted replica looks really cute.

Finally, I drape one of the blankets I crocheted along the edge of the bed. Once I'm happy with the arrangement, I put my phone camera self-timer on and quickly get into place—lying on my bed with all of the crochet things surrounding me. This time, instead of looking directly at the phone, I look off to the side and try to make a dreamy expression. At some point, Poppy comes in and jumps on the bed, but I don't bother moving her. Poppy is my best friend these days, so she can stay. It takes a few tries but eventually I get the shot I want.

Once again, I take a few minutes to edit the photo and print it out. Then I look at the two prints side by side.

I love them. Looking at them makes me more excited than any of my theater photos. I can already see how I can edit them better to make the colors pop more.

What if I took more pictures of myself at my other happy places—at Get Crafty, in Mr. G's classroom, at the bubble tea place, at my favorite park? I could create this whole photo essay of self-portraits. It would be the most "me" thing I've ever created.

If I take the pictures quickly enough, I can probably get permission from Mr. G to change my photo essay topic.

But then I think about what other kids at school might say.

It's not only my anxiety that makes me feel different from my classmates. I *am* different. I don't care about social media, I don't take selfies, and I'd rather spend a Friday night crafting than texting.

But I like myself. I do. I just wish I felt more confident at school and didn't care what other people thought. Maybe then I would've been able to talk to other kids and make a new best friend when Elise moved on with Amelia.

I'd rather use the theater photos for the photography

club showcase. These self-portraits can be just for me.

I look at them again and wish I could send them to Elise. I bet, if we were still friends, she'd be impressed that I actually took a picture of myself, on purpose. She might even be proud.

If she didn't hate me.

# Twenty-Four

On Saturday afternoon, I walk into the local library and head straight for the study room that Elise reserved. She came by my locker yesterday to suggest we meet here to work on our photo essays. I was going to tell her that she could come over to my house, but I guess since we aren't friends, the library is a better idea.

Elise is already in the room when I get there. She has some photo prints spread out on the rectangular table. She also has a laptop open with some other photos on the screen. I don't recognize any of them, so I move closer to the screen to take a look.

"You took my advice," I say, once I realize what I'm looking at.

All of the pictures on the screen feature Sunny. One shows Sunny in her dog bed nook under the register, getting petted by a customer. She has the biggest pup smile on her face. Another shows her sitting in between two toddlers while they all listen to story time. It's really cute. Then there are a couple more with Sunny and the bookstore employees in a back room.

"Sunny makes the bookstore special, so she deserves to be the focus," Elise says. "I went there this morning to take these. I still need to edit them."

"They look great already," I say.

"Thanks for the idea."

I respond with a smile.

"What about you?" Elise asks. "Did you make any changes to your essay?"

I'm shocked. Elise is talking to me and acting like a real partner. It makes some of the tightness in my chest go away.

"Not really," I admit. "I'm not sure what else to do. Unless you have any ideas, I'm going to talk to Mr. G on Monday."

I pull out my photo folder and spread the prints out so

we can look at them again. That's when I realize that the two self-portraits I took in my room earlier that week are mixed in. I must've accidentally put them in the folder when I was looking through my theater photos. I try to snatch them up quickly, so Elise doesn't see them. But it's too late.

"What are these?" Elise is staring at the picture of me in front of my desk.

My heart starts to race. "Oh. Um, it's nothing." I hold out my hand so she can give it back, but she ignores me.

"Is this a new picture for your photo essay?"

I wish she would stop staring at it. "No. I was just experimenting with something in my room the other day. It's nothing." I gently pull the photo out of her hand.

"It's cool. Like the photos you see in articles showing behind the scenes of someone's life."

"You think so?"

"Yeah. I'm just surprised to see it because you said you don't like taking selfies." She pauses. "Unless you lied about that, too."

Ouch.

"That wasn't a lie," I say. "I don't like selfies. But I had an idea, so I thought I'd try it out. I'm not bringing these to photography club. They weren't even supposed to be in this folder."

"What idea?"

Elise seems genuinely curious, but I'm still nervous to share. What if she makes fun of me? It's not like she hasn't been in my room and seen all this stuff but panic still rises in my throat. My brain tells me to grab all the photo prints and run out of here.

But if I stay, maybe opening up will help fix things between us.

"You gave me the idea," I finally say.

"I did?"

"Yeah. It was your comment about my theater photo essay. You thought I chose my topic because I'm really into theater. It made me want to take pictures of what I'm *actually* really into, which is, you know, crafting."

"I always thought your crafts were great," Elise says. "You're so creative. Can I see the pictures again?"

I hesitate but place them back on the table.

"They're so cute. And I like how you took this one from above. We had the same idea."

"Thanks."

"You should take more photos like this and make them your photo essay. I mean, your other pictures are good, but like you said, these show more of who you are. I bet Mr. G would like them."

It's not Mr. G that I'm worried about. I know he'll be

supportive. He never judges us, or what we choose to photograph. But what about everyone else?

"I'll think about it," I lie.

Suddenly, I realize something even more important than our photo essays. This is the first time Elise and I have had a calm, friendly conversation since before the last full moon.

I pull my locket out from below my collar and open it. Elise notices what I'm doing and grabs hers, too. But the big and little hands on my clock are still rotating around and around.

I slump back in my chair.

"What?" Elise asks.

"This is the first time we haven't, like, fought," I say. "So, I thought it might . . . But nothing's changed."

"Oh."

"I know you want to reverse the spell," I say. "And I promise I want to, too."

"I want to believe you," she says. "But I don't know if I can trust you. After everything that's happened."

Her words feel like a punch in the gut.

"Well, what do you think we need to do to 'unite'?" I ask after an awkward moment of silence.

Elise shrugs. "I wish I knew. In fantasy novels, sometimes the main character has to learn a lesson before they can get through the final battle. Like, they have to go through some sort of change or shift in perspective. Then that helps them succeed."

"This isn't a fantasy novel," I say, though now that I know magic is real and all, it may as well be.

"I know. But maybe there's something we still need to learn."

"If that's true, then why didn't Daphne tell us that?" I ask. "She didn't say anything about a lesson."

Elise shrugs again. "It's just a thought."

"What does 'unite' mean anyway?" I ask. "It's so vague."

Elise doesn't answer, so we sit there quietly for another minute.

"What if our clocks don't stop rotating in time for the next full moon?" I ask. "Like, what if we fail? Does that ever happen in the books you read?"

"Sometimes the main character fails," Elise says. "But they usually get something else out of it, so there's still a happy ending."

I think about that. If we can't reverse the spell, could we still have a happy ending?

I'd still be without a best friend. And even worse, I'd have to live with knowing that my selfish decision is why Elise can't get her time back. She doesn't trust me, and if I can't get this spell reversed, she never will.

* * *

I spend all of Sunday shooting more self-portraits. It's the first time since the time jump that I lose myself in a creative project, and it feels amazing. I take some good shots at my favorite stores downtown, like Get Crafty. I also go to my favorite park and take a portrait in front of a patch of spring wildflowers.

More than once, I want to text Elise and show her my pictures. But I know she doesn't want to hear from me.

Sitting on my bed with my laptop on my lap, I adjust the exposure and lighting in my photos, and I try to think about what else I might need to learn in order to reverse the spell. I already know that I messed things up for Elise, and I want to make it right. What other shift do I need to make?

Whatever it is, I need to figure it out soon.

I get up to grab prints from my printer, and as I lean over, the locket falls from underneath my shirt and gently swings back and forth. I grab on to it to steady it and can almost feel the clock's soft tick tick tick.

Time is running out.

# Twenty-Five

When I walk into the bathroom at the beginning of lunch period on Monday, Ivy and Melinda are standing in front of the sink mirrors. They're laughing about something as Melinda reapplies lip gloss and Ivy pulls her long black hair into a bun. They ignore me as I go into the first stall.

I think about what Melinda did to Elise. How could she be so cruel to someone who considered her a friend? Melinda doesn't know how lucky she was to have not one, but two best friends. If I was in her position, I would never let jealousy mess everything up.

But who am I to judge? My grandma likes to say that

"hurt people hurt people." Maybe Melinda is just inse-
cure, like me. Maybe one day, she'll realize she made a
huge mistake.

I hear someone else flush in the stall next to me. I
didn't realize anyone else other than Ivy and Melinda
were in here.

I walk out of my stall at the same time as the girl in the
neighboring one. That's when I see that it's Elise.

The room fills with uncomfortable silence when Elise
and I go over to the sinks to wash our hands. Ivy and
Melinda don't look at Elise, and Elise doesn't look at me.

I'm about to disappear back into the hallway when
Elise says, "You know, for the last few weeks I've been
trying to figure out how to be friends with you both
again."

Melinda scoffs but Elise keeps going. "I was desperate
to fix what happened between us."

I'm too curious to leave now, so I linger near the bathroom exit.

"You mean, how you lied about me?" Ivy asks. She
sounds truly hurt.

"No. How *Melinda* lied," Elise says.

Melinda gives an exaggerated eye roll. "You don't
know what you're talking about."

"I do, and you know it," Elise says, staring right at her.

"Maybe everyone else believes that I made up that rumor, but you and I know the truth. And I'm pretty sure, deep down, Ivy knows it, too."

Ivy shakes her head. "Melinda wouldn't do that to me."

"But you really think I would?" Elise asks, and now she's the one who sounds sad. "I know we hadn't been friends for that long, but I thought you knew me better than that. I was wrong."

Elise slowly exhales. "It doesn't matter if you believe me because I don't want our friendship back anymore. It was never real anyway. A real friend wouldn't stab me in the back—or believe I'd do something so terrible."

Then she looks at Ivy. "But you should think about whether you're friends with the right person."

Ivy opens her mouth to respond, but nothing comes out.

Elise, looking shaky but determined, turns around and storms out of the bathroom.

I turn toward the sinks again. Melinda's looking at Ivy like she's worried Ivy might believe Elise. Ivy looks confused.

I don't stick around to see what Ivy and Melinda do or say next. I need to find Elise. Out in the hall, I see her heading toward the cafeteria.

"Elise, wait!" I walk quickly to catch up with her.

She pauses and turns toward me.

"That was amazing," I say. "How you confronted them."

Elise exhales like she's just as surprised by what she did. She looks pleased with herself, and she should be. "I had to say something, since I don't know if Dream Elise ever did."

"I'm proud of you," I say.

She flashes a smile. "Thanks."

"Do you think that could've, you know . . ." I motion to her locket. "I'm scared to look."

"I don't know."

I watch as Elise opens her locket. It's clear from the look on her face that nothing's changed. She faces it toward me, and I can see the tiny hands still steadily moving.

I don't bother checking mine because I know it'll be the same.

For the rest of the day, I can't stop thinking about what Elise did. She's so brave. For standing up to Melinda and Ivy. For sticking with photography club even though it's outside her comfort zone. And for how she's handled everything since the time jump.

She's the brave one and I'm the coward. I'm always hiding in the shadows, too scared to talk to other kids at school because I'm worried they'll judge me. I chose a "safe" photo essay topic. And then I took the easy road and performed a spell to make a best friend.

I don't want to be that person anymore.

And the more I think about it, the more I'm certain that if Elise and I are going to "unite" enough to reverse this spell, it's going to be up to me to change. I've got to be the reason why the clock hands are still moving. I got us into this, and I'm the one who will get us out.

If I can figure this out in time for the next full moon.

There's one change I know I can make right away. After photography club, when everyone else has left his classroom, I stay behind to talk to Mr. G.

"Do you have a question, Cora?" he asks when he notices I'm still here.

"Actually, I need to talk to you about my photo essay." I take a deep breath. "I know it's last minute, but I want to switch topics. I . . . have an even better idea."

"Oh?" Mr. G says. "What's that?"

I glance at his "Creativity Takes Courage" poster before reaching into my backpack and pulling out a folder of my self-portrait prints. The ones I've been editing and printing out at home. I brought them to school in case I got the chance to show them to Elise.

My hands shake a little as I hand the folder to Mr. G.

But I don't turn back. It's about time I do something brave.

Before I shoot the rest of my new photo essay, I make a list of the locations, what equipment I'll need to bring, and what I want to wear in each shot. I also asked Mr. G to borrow the DSLR camera for the upcoming weekend. Thankfully, nobody else needs to use it, since I'm the only one starting her essay over from scratch. The showcase is less than two weeks away, so I need to work fast.

# Twenty-Six

I'm looking over my photo essay plans a few nights later when Mom walks into my room with a basket of clean laundry. She sets it next to my closet for me to put away.

"How's it going in here?" she asks.

"Pretty good."

"Good." Mom sits on my bed and pets Poppy. "I had coffee with Elise's mom today."

Oh no. Did Elise's mom say we weren't friends anymore? I brace myself for Mom's disappointment.

But Mom says, "We were talking about how nice it is that you and Elise reconnected at school. Now her mom and I have reconnected, too."

Wow. That must mean Elise hasn't said anything to her parents either. Probably because she's expecting us to get back to last October, when it won't matter anymore.

"You can invite her over anytime," Mom adds.

If I do, Elise won't want to come. Not unless she thinks it'll help us reverse this spell. And once it is reversed, she'll go back to not remembering I exist.

"What's wrong?" Mom asks. "You seem sad."

I'm about to say nothing's wrong, like I always do. But maybe this is another way that I need to change. I should stop hiding my true feelings from my parents.

I take a deep breath and sit next to her on my bed. "You know how I used to feel anxious about talking to kids at school?"

Mom nods.

I never felt anxious until the pandemic lockdown at the end of the third grade. When I was allowed to go back to school in person for fourth grade, at first, I was anxious about getting sick. But then when Elise stopped hanging out with me, my confidence plummeted, and I became too scared to talk to other kids. It was like I didn't know how anymore.

When my parents noticed that I wasn't spending time with friends, they talked to my pediatrician about how to help. She suggested things like deep breathing and journaling and practicing friendship skills like conversation starters.

Something about my parents knowing I was struggling made me feel even more ashamed. So, even though the strategies don't always help, I've been pretending that they do.

"I haven't been totally honest," I say. "The truth is, I don't really have friends."

Mom's forehead wrinkles. "What about Elise?"

"We were friends, but then . . ." I pause while I try to figure out how to explain this without mentioning the spell. "We got into a fight."

"I had no idea. And her mom didn't say anything either . . ."

"It kind of just happened," I say.

"Well, what about your art class friends?" Mom asks. "And the friends from photography club?"

I shake my head. "I've been too . . . anxious . . . to say more than a few words to those kids. To any kids at school, really."

Mom looks more worried now. "How long have you been feeling this way? I thought you were doing better."

"I hated that you and Dad were worrying about me, so I started pretending everything was fine."

"Oh, honey." Her face crumples into the saddest expression I've ever seen on her, which makes me feel guilty.

"It's our job to worry about you. We want to make sure you're okay." She reaches over and wraps her arm around my shoulder. "I think we should make an appointment with your pediatrician. Talking with a therapist might be the best next step."

"Okay."

"I'm so glad you finally told me," Mom says.

My eyes well up a little and I blink back the tears.

"I'm glad I did, too," I say.

"We'll get through this. And you know you can always talk to me and Dad. It's what we're here for." She squeezes me again. "In the meantime, I hope you can work things out with Elise. You're both such sweet kids and have shared history."

"I'll see," I say with a shrug.

Mom stands up and goes to my doorway. "I'll come back in a little while to say good night."

"Okay."

Mom leaves and I lie back on my bed, feeling lighter and relieved after finally opening up to her.

Then I realize something. When this spell gets reversed and I'm back in October, I'll have to have this entire conversation about my anxiety with Mom again. . . .

*Ugh . . .*

But when I think about how Mom just looked at me—not judging me at all—talking to her about this again doesn't feel so scary.

I get up to put away my laundry. While I'm doing that, I think again about the pictures I've taken so far for my new photo essay. I like the ones I took at the park and bubble tea shop, but not as much as the ones where I'm showing off my crafts. Maybe I should do self-portraits holding different things I've made.

I peer around my room to see what crafts I'd want to showcase—my crocheted cupcake, my "creativity takes courage" handwritten sign. Then my eyes land on the book nook frame. It'd be cool if I held it up in a photo or positioned it on my bookshelf and stood next to it. But that means I'd have to finish it fast. I still don't know what its theme should be.

The last thing Mom said before she left is still ringing in my ears. *I hope you can work things out with Elise.*

I really hope I can, too. Not only to be able to reverse the spell. But because she is a great person, and I want to be the kind of friend who deserves her friendship.

Maybe I can re-create something from our friendship in the book nook. A scene from when we were younger? I could make it look like the beach from my movie night memory. Or maybe I should create the inside of Sunny's Books and have all of Elise's favorite fantasy titles on the shelves. I could even make a miniature Sunny replica. I'd make one of the inside of Daphne's Delights, since it's such a pretty store, but I don't think reminding Elise of the place where I got the spell would help win her over.

My hand goes to my locket around my neck.

And then I think of a perfect idea.

## Twenty-Seven

*It's finally time for our* photography club showcase, and I might throw up. I know people say that a lot when they're nervous, but this time it's true. I've never felt so sick to my stomach.

It took me ten hours over multiple nights to finish designing and building all of the pieces I needed for the book nook. Thankfully, my parents were willing to help me pay for all the supplies, since I went over my budget. I finally finished the book nook in time to take a picture with it. I took the rest of the photos I needed with my other crafts.

Then, at last week's photography club meeting, everybody printed their final photos, and we mounted them on pieces of thick white cardstock.

I still hadn't told Elise that I changed my photo essay topic. I wanted to wait until the last possible second, so it'd be a surprise. I worked at a different desk on the opposite side of the room. If she cared that I wasn't sitting next to her like normal, she didn't say anything.

I showed them all to Mr. G, though, of course, and as I guessed, he liked them—even more than my theater photos! He even asked to see a close-up of my book nook once I told him I created it myself. He was super impressed, which filled me with pride.

Earlier this afternoon, the other photography club kids and I brought our mounted prints to the gym. Mr. G had set up several art-display panels around the perimeter. They looked like black rectangles on wheels. Mr. G put us in alphabetical order and assigned each of us to a panel to hang our prints.

To make it look even more official, Mr. G printed small cards with our names and the titles of our photo essays. I decided to name mine "The Artist and Her Art." Mr. G placed the title cards to the side of our photographs. Once everything was set up, it really did look like an art gallery installation.

My photos were on the very first panel when you walked into the gym, next to Alex Carrera's. That meant my face would be the first thing everyone saw when they came to the showcase. Me, ten different times. Plus, all of the things I'd created over the years, when I wasn't hanging out with my nonexistent friends. They might as well be getting a glimpse into my soul.

Mr. G ended the meeting early so we would have enough time to get ready at home, before coming back at night for the showcase opening. But before we left, he told us to check out each other's pictures. It was the first time we all got to see each other's entire photo essays, so we all walked around and admired them. I saw that Elise named hers "The Best Bookstore Dog."

"You changed your topic," Elise said once she got to mine.

"Yeah." I held my breath while she stood in front of my prints and took them all in. I put the book nook photo last because I'm most proud of it. I watched as Elise's eyes landed on it.

She quietly gasped and leaned closer to the picture to get a better look.

The book nook shows a glimpse of Main Street downtown. The paved road in the middle, the brick sidewalks along the sides, and a few storefronts. I included Sunny's

Books, Get Crafty, and, of course, Daphne's Delights. The storefronts have tiny doors and windows, along with their signs. I also added some plants and flowers to the scene to give it some more color, and draped fairy lights around the border so it can light up at night. It's not an exact replica of Main Street but I think I captured its spirit.

None of that was the best part. I decided to add us to the book nook—me and Elise. I took two wooden peg dolls and painted them to look like us, then placed them in the middle of the scene. I even used yarn to create Elise's bun and my twists. If you look closely, you can see our matching lockets that I painted around our necks.

Elise turned to look at me. "You put us into your book nook?"

I smiled. "Yes. You were the one who inspired me to take more self-portraits and make my photo essay more personal, so I decided to re-create us in the book nook."

"It's really nice," Elise said. "I can't believe you added all of those tiny details. I wish I could see it in person."

"Come see it anytime."

"We must've rubbed off on each other," Elise said next. "Because now I like taking pictures of other things more. I'm glad you encouraged me to stick with photography club. I know it's not perfect, but I'm really proud of my photo essay."

"You did a great job," I said.

Now it's a couple hours later, and we're back at school. It's always weird coming here after hours for evening activities. With no daylight streaming in through the windows, the hallways look darker and feel more ominous.

I was going to wear a black dress tonight, since that felt art exhibit-y, but then I remembered that I'm not here to blend in or hide. So, I switched to a yellow dress with a sequined bodice and tulle skirt that I wore to a family wedding last summer. It's probably too dressy for tonight, but I'm okay with that. I even had my mom take my twists out and we did a quick wash and go. I don't normally let my natural curls out for school, and I'm a little nervous about it, but they look nice, and I feel pretty.

When my parents and I walk into the gym to join everyone, I immediately spot Elise. She's here with her parents and siblings, plus a few of her siblings' friends. Her outfit is a simple white shirt and black skirt, with a pop of color in her red flats. She's still wearing her locket, and so am I.

Mom notices Elise and her family, too, and gives a wave.

Mr. G calls for everyone's attention a minute later. Everyone gathers closer to hear what he has to say. The other photography club kids are standing with their parents and siblings. Some other kids from school are here, too, to support their friends.

"Thank you all for coming tonight," Mr. G says into a microphone. "Before you view our students' amazing photo essays, I want to thank a few people." He goes on to thank the Connecticut Arts Foundation for a grant that he used to buy a lot of our supplies, like the photo printer in his classroom, the DSLR camera he lets us borrow, and the display panels we're using tonight.

"I also have to thank my incredible students," Mr. G says. "You've all created inspiring photo essays, and it's an honor to celebrate them tonight. Thank you for putting in the work. Now, tonight is just the start of the showcase. Throughout the week, all Chester Middle School students will get the chance to visit the showcase during their art periods. We want to make sure everyone gets to view these incredible photo essays."

My chest tightens. This means that by the end of the week, every single kid at school will have seen my self-portraits and crafts. The thought makes me want to throw up even more.

But then I remind myself why I'm doing this. I'm tired of hiding in my shell. I'm proud of my photo essay and all of the crafts. If someone doesn't like them, that's their problem—not mine.

"Before we enjoy the rest of our reception, do any of my photographers want to say anything?" Mr. G asks.

I look around, but nobody raises their hand.

"Okay, then. Enjoy the photo essays, and feel free to grab some refreshments as well from the table near the entrance."

"Wait!" The word flies out of me like vomit, and before I can stop myself, I squeeze my way to where Mr. G is standing. "I'll say something, if that's okay."

Mr. G grins. "Of course." He hands me the microphone and steps to the side.

I look out at the crowd, at all the eyes on me, and freeze. *What am I doing?* My heart beats so fast, it vibrates my eardrums. I think about saying "never mind" and handing the mic back to Mr. G.

But then my eyes land on my parents, who've moved to the front to watch me. They look confused—probably because this is so out of character for me—but there's also encouragement and pride in their faces.

I can't see Elise from here, but I hope she's paying attention.

After a deep breath, I lift the mic to my mouth. "I'm Cora Burroughs. Um, I just want to say something about my photo essay, before you all go see it. I actually started out with a totally different topic, about our local theater.

227

But . . . a friend . . . I mean, classmate . . . inspired me to change it to something more meaningful to me."

I pause to take another breath. My nerves are making me sweat.

"Ever since I got to this school," I continue, "and even before that, I've kept to myself. I've hidden in the shadows. Photography club was the only club I joined, and it was because I knew I could hide behind my camera. I was scared that if I stood out, if I put my true self out there, I'd be judged. Or made fun of."

I'm shaking but force myself to keep going. "But I've realized I can't keep doing this. People won't always get you . . . and that's okay. You just have to find the people who do. And you have to put yourself out there to find them. I finally had a person like that back in my life, but then I did something that messed it all up. I really regret that."

Looking out at the faces staring at me, I can tell they have no idea what I'm talking about. Except for Mom, who nods along with my every word. But that's okay. There's only one person who needs to understand.

"Anyway, I learned that I shouldn't hide myself anymore. So, with my new photo essay topic, I put it all out there. It's all me. I hope you like it. And I want to thank that classmate. Their bravery inspired me." I look over at

Mr. G and hold the mic back out to him. "Um, that's it."

He smiles and takes it. There's a small round of applause, which only lasts a few seconds, but feels like an eternity.

"Thank you, Cora," Mr. G says. "Everyone, please enjoy the showcase."

"Honey, that was beautiful," Mom says as she comes over to hug me. "I know how hard it must've been to speak in front of all of these people. I'm so proud of you."

Dad nods in agreement. "I can't wait to see your pictures. I loved the theater ones, but I know I'll love these more."

I lead them over to my photo essay display.

When we get there, many others are already looking at it.

"This is really cool," one kid says when he notices me.

I grin. "Thanks."

"Did you make all of those projects?" Shay, Elise's sister, asks.

When I say yes, she says, "Wow. You're an incredible artist. When you're famous one day, that friendship bracelet you made me will be worth a lot of money." She laughs and winks at me.

I beam.

I get a few other compliments from kids and parents.

Even though I don't need to hear them to feel proud of myself, each one fills me up with joy.

Then I feel a hand on my arm. When I turn, I see Elise.

"Can we talk?" she asks.

"Sure."

This is it. The moment of truth. I know I've changed, but is it enough to gain Elise's trust back?

I tell my parents I'll be right back and follow Elise out of the gym.

# Twenty-Eight

Elise and I walk down the hall to the benches next to the school's main entrance and sit.

"By the way, I barely recognized you tonight," Elise says. "That's such a pretty dress, and I love your hair like that."

I grin. "Thanks."

"You're welcome." She pauses, and then says, "So, were you talking about me up there?"

"What? No," I say. "I was talking about Poppy. She is truly an inspirational cat."

Elise narrows her eyes at me. "But you said 'class-mate' . . ."

I laugh. "I know. That was a bad joke. Of course, I was talking about you."

"Oh." She smiles. "I thought so."

"After you stood up to Melinda and Ivy in the bathroom, I realized that I need to do the same," I say. "Just in my own way."

"I still can't believe I confronted them," Elise says. "I was, like, buzzing, for the rest of the day."

"It was great," I say.

"Thanks." Then Elise says, "I've been thinking. I'm still not happy the time jump happened, but there have been silver linings. You were right about Melinda and Ivy all along. They weren't true friends. But I was so focused on having best friends again after Amelia moved that I couldn't see it. I didn't want to lose more friends. But it's okay to lose people who aren't really there for you. I don't know if I would've realized that if all of this hadn't happened."

"I feel the same way," I say. "Like, I want to go back to October, but I also don't want to lose what I've learned. I don't want to go back to caring so much about what other people think that I close myself off."

"Totally."

I want to ask if she thinks we could still be friends after

all of this is fixed, but I'm scared of how she'll answer.

"So, you don't hate me?" I ask instead.

Elise shakes her head. "No. You said you didn't do the spell to hurt me, and I believe you." She laughs. "I guess I should be flattered that you wanted our friendship back that much."

"Do you think . . . once the spell is reversed . . . we can start over?" I ask, my voice tentative. "The two of us, being friends?"

"Sure," Elise says. "I'd like that."

It feels like a weight has lifted off me. But then I feel a jolt on my sternum.

"Ow!" I say at the same time that Elise says, "Ouch!"

I put my hand there to figure out what hurt and realize that my locket is pulsing.

"What the heck!" Elise says as she rips her locket off.

I do the same. Once it's off, the locket is no longer vibrating.

Elise's eyes are wide. "Do you think . . . ?"

"It has to be," I answer.

"Let's open them together," Elise says.

"On the count of three," I say. "One . . ."

"Two . . . ," Elise says.

"Three!" we say at the same time.

We open our lockets right next to each other and stare inside them. Both clock hands have stopped moving. They're all pointed toward the twelve. Toward midnight.

Elise and I glance at each other with wide eyes. We don't even need to say anything because we both know what this means.

"We have to go to Daphne's Delights right now." Elise stands up. "We only have two days until the full moon."

I pull out my phone and check the actual time. It's 7:34 p.m. The store closes in less than thirty minutes.

"How will we convince our parents to leave the showcase and bring us there?" I ask.

"I already know my parents will say no," Elise says with a sigh. "We'll have to go right after school tomorrow, then."

"It's a plan."

When Elise and I get to Daphne's Delights after school the next day, we expect the store to be empty like the last time. But Daphne is busy helping a customer.

She notices us right away since the bells on the door crash especially loudly when we burst inside.

"Hi, Cora. Hi, Elise," Daphne says with her usual calming smile. "I'll be with you in just a minute."

We nod at her, stand near the window, and wait.

"Maybe she'll like a beginner pack of tarot cards?" Daphne says to the customer, a man who looks like he's in his twenties.

"Yes. I think she'll love that," the man says.

Elise nudges me, and in a quiet voice, says, "Hopefully Daphne made the spell reversal kit, and we can meet tomorrow night to do it."

I nod. "I was thinking, maybe we should ask her to help us perform the spell, so it's done right. Like we could come here tomorrow night."

"Do you think the spell needs to happen at midnight?" Elise asks.

"I did the original spell close to midnight," I say. "If Daphne's willing to help, we could always sneak out again to meet her."

"True," Elise says. "Let's definitely ask her."

"Friends!"

We both jump at Daphne's voice. She's standing in front of us now, smiling.

The other customer is putting his wallet back into his pocket up at the register. He thanks Daphne again before leaving the store.

"Did your lockets tell you it's time?" Daphne asks, though I have a feeling she already knows the answer.

"Yes," Elise says. "The hands stopped moving, and we

talked everything out yesterday. We're finally united."

"Wonderful," Daphne says. "I knew you'd get there."

"Is the spell reversal kit ready?" I ask.

"It is." Daphne nods.

"We were thinking," I say. "Can we come back tomorrow, the night of the full moon, and do the reversal here? So, you can help us make sure we're doing it right?"

"Hmm. It would be best to do it at midnight," Daphne says. "Though my shop closes at eight."

"We know," I say. "But we hoped you'd make an exception for us. We can make it back here before midnight."

"We promise," Elise says.

Daphne's mouth twists as she thinks, and I hold my breath. "Fine. I suppose I can come back here in time. As long as you're sure you can get here safely."

We both nod.

"Thank you!" Elise says. "Should we bring anything with us?"

"Just you and your lockets," Daphne says. "I'll have everything else."

I instinctively wrap my hand around my locket. "Will we have to get rid of the lockets for the reversal to work? I want to keep mine."

Daphne looks at me, and her eyebrows slowly rise.

"Oh dear. I'm afraid I may not have made certain things clear enough earlier . . ."

"Made what clear?" Elise asks.

"When we reverse the spell, and you go back to . . . what was it, October?"

Elise and I both nod.

"You won't have the lockets anymore," Daphne continues. "And I can't guarantee that you will remember the spell or time jump at all. Most likely, you will go back to that night, and wake up the next morning as if nothing happened. You might feel like you've just had the strangest dream, but just like with most dreams, you won't be able to remember what it was about."

"But . . . I want to remember everything," I say.

I think of the silver linings, as Elise called them. How the time jump led to Ivy and Melinda no longer being friends with Elise, and that led to Elise seeing their true colors and standing up to them. Which led me to realize that I need to be brave and try harder to make more friends. I finally opened up to my parents about my anxiety. If I go back to October, I won't remember any of this?

Not only that, but if Elise and I don't have these memories, how can we start over and try to be friends? Elise will still be besties with Melinda and Ivy. I'll still be alone.

I glance at Elise and from the look on her face, I can

tell she's trying to work this out in her head, too.

"What about you?" I ask her.

"I want to remember, too," she says.

"Does that mean you don't want to reverse the spell, after all?" Daphne asks.

"No," I say. "I mean, I don't know."

"I have a question," Elise says. "Let's say we don't reverse the spell. That means it'll still have some control over us, right? Like, it could still affect our lives or make us jump in time again?"

"Well, now that you're united and friends, the magic shouldn't need to do anything further," Daphne says.

"Could that change if we stopped being friends?" I ask. "I'm not saying that would happen, but what if it did?"

"Here's the thing," Daphne says. "Magic can be messy, and nothing is for certain. If we do the spell reversal, I can't guarantee that you will remember everything—like I said. And if we don't reverse the spell, I can't guarantee that its magic won't continue to impact you in some way."

I look at Elise. "What do you think?"

"If we reverse the spell and don't remember everything that's happened, things could still turn out the same," Elise says. "I thought my lost time self might've done things differently than I would, but I don't know if that's true."

Daphne chimes in. "The version of you that experienced October through April was still you. It wouldn't act differently."

"Interesting . . . ," Elise says, her head tilting to the side. She's probably remembering what happened with Melinda and Ivy during her lost time.

"So, if everything ends up the same after the spell reversal, then Cora and I could still come back as friends," Elise says.

"I wish I could tell you for certain," Daphne says. "But I can't."

"Trying to figure this out is making my brain hurt," Elise says.

"Mine, too," I say.

"You have one more day to think about it," Daphne says. "But you need to decide together."

Elise and I look at each other. So much was at stake— our pasts, and our futures. This couldn't be a split-second decision.

How were we going to choose?

# Part Three

## Elise

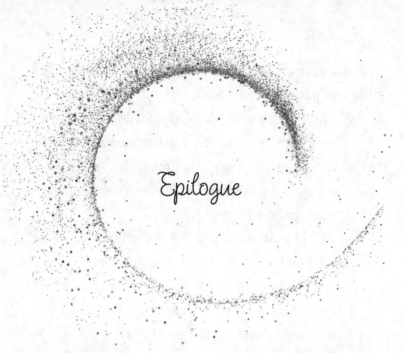

# Epilogue

Down in the basement, there are three sleeping bags lined up in a row. I pull pillows off the couch to make the floor comfier. The coffee table has bowls of my favorite movie snacks: M&M's, Sour Patch Kids, and popcorn. The TV mounted on the wall is ready to play *Spirited Away*.

Amelia skips down the stairs holding a package of Oreos and a big bag of cheddar popcorn. "Your mom gave me these to bring down."

"Nice!" I take them from her and add them to our snack pile on the coffee table.

Amelia has been in town for the last week. Her parents flew back to Connecticut with her and her younger sister to spend a few weeks with their grandparents. They live a couple towns over from here.

Whenever Amelia hasn't been with her family, she's been over here. We've been making up for lost time, holding reading marathons, sharing gossip, riding bikes, and hanging out downtown. It's been so nice to be back in the same place with my best friend.

Amelia plops down on the couch and curls her feet under her. "What time is Cora going to be here?"

"Should be any minute."

I invited Cora to sleep over since we haven't seen each other much since summer started. She's been going to an art camp.

It's been a couple of months since that day in Daphne's Delights when Cora and I had to decide whether to reverse the spell or take our chances with the spell's magic hanging over us. We really wanted to reverse the spell but also keep our memories—and our friendship.

We didn't have long to choose so we decided to go with our guts. Our guts told us that we didn't want to lose our friendship, and everything we'd learned about ourselves from this experience. We realized those were worth more than our lost time.

So, in the end, we chose each other.

Neither of us knows what the future holds. But as long

as we commit to always being friends, no matter what, the spell will never need to intervene.

There's a knock on the top of the basement steps. "Hello?"

It's Cora.

"Come down!" I shout.

Cora walks down the stairs wearing a sundress with . . .

"Are those *books* all over your dress?" I immediately ask.

"Yes! You like it?" She puts down two shopping bags and twirls around.

"Of course!" I say. "I kinda want one for myself."

I glance around Cora's neck to see if she wore her locket. But I don't see it. I'm not wearing mine either. Right now, it's tucked away in a box in my nightstand drawer. At the end of the school year, Cora and I agreed not to tell anyone about the spell or the time jump, since nobody would believe us anyway.

Even Amelia still thinks we became friends because of photography club.

Amelia and Cora say hi to each other, and Cora sits next to her on the couch.

"What's in the bag?" I ask.

"Oh." Cora gets back up and pulls a couple of blank

canvases out of it. "I brought over some paint supplies. I thought if we got bored, we could create our own painting party. I did this last weekend with Emily, my friend from art camp, and it was so fun. They have videos we can follow online." Cora pauses. "But only if you want. We totally don't have to."

"That sounds really fun," Amelia says.

"Yeah," I agree. "Let's do it. But maybe in the kitchen, where my parents won't care if we make a mess."

"Okay, but first I have something else." Cora pulls something wrapped in Bubble Wrap from the second bag, and hands it to me. "For you."

"What is this?" I ask.

"Open it!" Cora says.

I carefully remove the Bubble Wrap and reveal . . . the book nook that Cora made for her photo essay. The one portraying downtown, with the two of us wearing our lockets in the center.

"You're giving this to me?" I ask.

Cora nods. "I made a second one already—a replica of my bedroom, with a tiny Poppy and everything." She pulls out her phone and shows us a picture. It's adorable.

"I thought you could keep this one on your bookshelf," Cora says. "And then I can see it when I come over."

"Thank you!" I give Cora a hug.

"Wow," Amelia says, looking closely at the book nook details. "This is so cool."

"Do you want me to make one for you?" Cora asks. "I can make it look like the inside of a comic shop, or a scene from one of your favorite graphic novels."

Amelia grins. "That would be amazing!"

They immediately start brainstorming ideas.

Later, we go upstairs and find a video showing us how to paint a night sky with fireflies. Even though we're all working on the same steps, my painting looks sort of wonky. Amelia's looks pretty good, and Cora's looks just like the one from the video. But hanging out painting together is the best part.

After we've cleaned everything up, Mom orders us pizza, which we eat in the basement along with all the other snacks.

We talk for a while instead of watching the movie, and then eventually get ready for bed. We turn off the main lights and turn on a starry night-light, which animates the ceiling with shadows and stars. It kind of reminds me of the ceiling at Daphne's Delights.

As we settle into our sleeping bags, I turn to look at Cora. She's whispering animatedly to Amelia about gossip from her art camp, and Amelia giggles back. I sigh happily and snuggle deeper into my blankets.

Tomorrow, I'll wake up in the morning in this exact spot. Everything will be the same. And yet completely different from last October. There's a magic to it all—to this new friendship between the three of us—but this time, it's different. This time, it's magic that we *chose*, that didn't involve any fancy spells. It belongs to us. It's real.

# Acknowledgments

This book would not be what it is without the help of my incredible editor, Mabel Hsu. Mabel, thank you for being so enthusiastic about my original idea and for your inspired suggestions during our brainstorming calls. It was fun to stretch my writing skills with this book, and your guidance throughout this process was invaluable!

I also must thank Lorien Lawrence, who was like a mentor while I wrote all of the magical scenes. Thank you for your advice and encouragement—and for taking me to a witchy shop in Connecticut for inspiration!

I'm blown away by the cover, so huge thanks to Audrey Sakho for the gorgeous illustration, and to Laura Mock and Amy Ryan for the design.

To the rest of my team at HarperCollins—Kristen Eckhardt, Erin DeSalvatore, Mark Rifkin, Sabrina Abballe, Sammy Brown, Patty Rosati, Mimi Rankin, Christina Carpino, Josie Dallam, Kerry Moynagh, and Dan Janeck—I appreciate all of your hard work and dedication.

Thank you to agent extraordinaire, Alex Slater, as well as the Sanford J. Greenburger Associates and Trident Media Group teams.

As always, I want to thank my husband, daughter, family, and friends for their unwavering support.

To the teachers, librarians, booksellers, and parents fighting the good fight to ensure all kids have the freedom to read all kinds of books: Thank you and stay strong. We need you!

Finally, to my young readers: Thank you for picking up this book. I know there are so many other ways to spend your time, so I'm thrilled that you chose to read this story. Keep reading and I will definitely keep writing for you!